EXT

| DATE | ISSUED TO |
|---|---|
| MT 4/7 | |
| CP 10 13 7/12 | |
| HG 20 7 B 4/21 | |
| HP 45 12/27 | |
| SX 122 1/16 | |
| CP 412 Y 23 | |
| JMS 3/26 | |
| M 385 19/7 | |
| | |
| | |
| | |
| | |

CAT. No. 23-115   PRINTED IN U.S.A.

**SPECIAL MESSAGE TO READERS**
This book is published under the auspices of
**THE ULVERSCROFT FOUNDATION**
(registered charity No. 264873 UK)
Established in 1972 to provide funds for research, diagnosis and treatment of eye diseases. Examples of contributions made are: —

A Children's Assessment Unit at
Moorfield's Hospital, London.

•

Twin operating theatres at the
Western Ophthalmic Hospital, London.

•

A Chair of Ophthalmology at the
Royal Australian College of Ophthalmologists.

•

The Ulverscroft Children's Eye Unit at the
Great Ormond Street Hospital For Sick Children,
London.

You can help further the work of the Foundation by making a donation or leaving a legacy. Every contribution, no matter how small, is received with gratitude. Please write for details to:

**THE ULVERSCROFT FOUNDATION,**
**The Green, Bradgate Road, Anstey,**
**Leicester LE7 7FU, England.**
**Telephone: (0116) 236 4325**

**In Australia write to:**
**THE ULVERSCROFT FOUNDATION,**
**c/o The Royal Australian and New Zealand**
**College of Ophthalmologists,**
**94-98 Chalmers Street, Surry Hills,**
**N.S.W. 2010, Australia**

# CRYPTIC CLUE

Fiona Graham, a physiotherapist, is found naked and lying face down in the swimming pool of Croxley Hall health farm where she worked. The coroner's verdict: accidental death by drowning. However, both her father and Golding, the forensic pathologist, disagree with his ruling. Inspector Roger Newton arrives with his assistant, Jane Warwick, to investigate a murder. But when Jane disappears, it's a race to unravel the 'Cryptic Clue' to her whereabouts — and the reason for Fiona's death.

*Books by Peter Conway
in the Linford Mystery Library:*

MURDER IN DUPLICATE
VICTIMS OF CIRCUMSTANCE
CRADLE SNATCH
ONE FOR THE ROAD

PETER CONWAY

# CRYPTIC CLUE

*Complete and Unabridged*

**LINFORD**
*Leicester*

First published in Great Britain
by Robert Hale Limited
London

First Linford Edition
published 2007
by arrangement with
Robert Hale Limited
London

Copyright © 1984 by Peter Conway
All rights reserved

British Library CIP Data

Conway, Peter, *1929* –
 Cryptic clue.—Large print ed.—
 Linford mystery library
 1. Murder—Investigation—Fiction 2. Health
 resorts—Fiction 3. Detective and mystery
 stories 4. Large type books
 I. Title
 823.9'14 [F]

ISBN 978–1–84617–713–2

Published by
F. A. Thorpe (Publishing)
Anstey, Leicestershire

Set by Words & Graphics Ltd.
Anstey, Leicestershire
Printed and bound in Great Britain by
T. J. International Ltd., Padstow, Cornwall

This book is printed on acid-free paper

# 1

Barbara Galton's eyes flicked open and she allowed herself the luxury of a half-smile as she saw that the luminous hands of the large alarm clock on her bedside table were showing precisely six-fifteen. She reached out to press the button on the top, stretched once and then got out of bed. She had forgotten exactly when the alarm had last gone off — it had certainly been a very long time ago — and it was a constant source of pride to her that her own internal clock should have been every bit as reliable as the mechanical version, waking her with unfailing regularity just five minutes before the time she had set on the dial.

She slipped off her pyjamas, had a quick wash and then stood for a moment looking at herself in the mirror. What if she was fifty-five and her hair had long since gone grey? She hadn't put on an ounce of weight in the last twenty years, her muscles were still as firm as those of someone half her age and she could still run three miles in well under half an hour, which she did every morning with her labrador, Rex, whatever the weather and whatever the season, between six-thirty and seven o'clock. Not for her jogging, which for most people amounted to no more than a tedious shuffle, little faster than a brisk walk, she genuinely ran, with a spring in her stride.

Barbara Galton was no masochist, though, and on some mornings it was an effort to leave the warmth of her bed, but not when it was June, the sky was clear and there were all the scents of a summer's day to savour. She put on her tracksuit and running shoes, went down the stairs, avoiding the steps that creaked, unlocked the front door and stood on the stone steps for a minute or two looking at the familiar view.

There weren't all that many people, she thought, who were able to combine an eminently satisfactory job with living in a magnificent country house. She had had some regrets about leaving St Gregory's, where she had been superintendent physiotherapist for nearly twenty years, but she had reached the top of her salary scale, she did have the long term future to consider, she was fed up with London and she didn't like the newly-appointed consultant in rheumatology and rehabilitation, who was very much tarred with the 'new broom' syndrome. What if the clientele at Croxley Hall was mostly elderly and extremely affluent, who, in the main, came to diet and work off a surfeit of good living, there were also those with physical illnesses, some of them even young, and the equipment was superb.

No, she didn't regret the move at all; not only was her pay half as much again as she had received before, but she delighted in the country and had developed a real interest in the old house and the chapel. The idea of writing a book about its history had come to her only a few months earlier and so far she had told no one except Pat Pennington and she had been most enthusiastic. Barbara Galton was also quite sure that the Chairman of the Board would also approve. Glover might have been a rough diamond, but he had certainly known what he had been doing when he had bought the Hall cheaply from the receiver after the unsuccessful girls' boarding school that had been there before had gone bankrupt. He had made it into a company, appointed an estate manager and before the clinic opened, the ugly appendages had been removed from the main buildings, restoring them to their original dimensions, the outdoor swimming pool had been retiled and fitted with solar heating, and many additional features added to the complex. The place had been an immediate success and looked like remaining one.

Barbara Galton went back inside and opened the door of the utility room, where Rex slept, to let him out. The labrador was far too well trained to have barked or scratched on the woodwork, but he had heard her come down and the unaccustomed wait had driven him wild with excitement. The animal hurtled out of the front door and careered around until her sharp whistle brought him to heel. She never varied her route — it was like an old and familiar friend; the distance was just right, most of it was on springy turf and it took her past all the old and new buildings, which always looked slightly different from day to day depending on the weather and the time of year.

She ran across the gravel drive, turned right on to the grass and made for the screen of trees a hundred yards ahead. The gymnasium, the small indoor pool and sauna were her real pride and joy; cunningly concealed both behind the trees and in a natural dip in the ground, they had been faced in Cotswold stone and blended in harmoniously with the surroundings. Barbara Galton never went past them without reflecting on what must have been their immense cost and comparing them with what she had had to put up with at St Gregory's. Having the latest and best equipment didn't necessarily lead to better treatment or a happier working atmosphere, of course, but it didn't do any harm either.

Circling further to the right, she passed

the cottage where Derek Milroy, the estate manager, and his wife lived and then over the five-bar gate and into the fields that had been rented to the Hockadays. For various reasons, most of which she preferred to keep to herself, Barbara Galton didn't like Milroy, but she had to admit that over some things he had done a good job, not least with the riding school. As part of the agreement with the Hockadays, horses were provided for the clients, lessons organised for those who wished and the facilities were available free for the staff; all of it looked good on the brochure and it didn't harm recruitment either.

The restoring of the chapel had been another of Milroy's inspired ideas. At first, she had heard, Glover had opposed it; he had no time for organised religion, the project wouldn't be cost effective and if a church really was required, something he doubted very much, there was a perfectly good one only a couple of miles away in the village, which the school had used previously and was now nearly always empty. Milroy hadn't been deterred; he organised an appeal for funds, got hold of a group of students from the Christian Union of Oxford University to work on it during the long summer vacation and in the end, even managed to persuade Glover to finance the heating and lighting when it became clear that the enterprise was proving of enormous publicity value. The man had become completely converted to the idea and arranged for one of his subsidiaries to carry out the work to the highest standard. There had been other benefits, too; a religious flavour added a certain cachet to the place and a bishop or two amongst the regular clients were an additional asset.

Barbara Galton's attention had wandered as she kept catching sight of the tower of the chapel through the trees and she failed to notice that Rex had disappeared, until, a few minutes later, she heard him bark and saw him standing at the beginning of the path that led through the rhododendrons in the direction of the swimming pool. She whistled, but for once the labrador failed to respond, gave another sharp bark and dashed back into the bushes, only to reappear seconds later, whining.

'What is it, boy?'

Barbara Galton ran up to the dog and then followed him as he trotted along the narrow path. Coming into sight of the pool, she glanced casually down at the water, took in the familiar white polystyrene bricks floating at one end and then saw something else. She didn't hesitate; almost without breaking stride, she launched herself into the pool, grabbed the girl who was floating face down on the water and frantically turned her over, hauled her to the shallow end and, taking her under the arms, dragged her backwards up the steps on to the surround.

She tried everything she knew, cardiac massage, mouth-to-mouth respiration, she even hung the girl's head over the side of the pool to see if she could drain some of the water out of her air passages, but after ten minutes, she knew that the situation was hopeless. Fiona Graham, one of the physiotherapists on her staff, was dead.

# 2

Bob Graham's mother hadn't liked Poms and neither did he. It wasn't just that his father, whom he'd never known, had been killed fighting for them at Gallipoli, or that he'd been taken prisoner himself by the Japanese in the Far East doing the same thing, it went far deeper than that. It was their accents, their wingeing, their unwillingness to work, it was . . . it was every bloody thing. He hadn't wanted Fiona to come to England and if he hadn't seen that magazine at the dentists in Sidney he would never have written to Glover and all this would . . .

His sour mood wasn't helping by having to open the hold-all at the security check, even though he knew that if he'd had any sense he would have been expecting it. At least the bloody man hadn't pulled anything out of it and his face had been devoid of expression as he put his hands in. If he'd so much as begun to snigger, Graham knew that he would have flattened him, Scotland Yard, or no bloody Scotland Yard.

'Yes, sir?'

The uniformed man at the desk looked up as he approached.

'I have an appointment with Inspector Newton — name of Graham.'

The man ran his finger down a list in front of himself. 'He's expecting you, sir. If you'd care to take the lift up to the fifth floor, someone will be waiting for you there.'

Some of Graham's prejudices — and in his heart of hearts he knew perfectly well that that was what they were — began to melt away when he was met outside the lift by a secretary who was wearing a crisp white blouse and a navy blue skirt and he was ushered straight into the inspector's office. The detective looked to be aged about forty and was tall and slim and although the Australian didn't care for the man's clipped way of speaking, at least his handshake was firm and dry.

'My assistant, Jane Warwick.'

Graham nodded towards the rather

plump girl, who didn't look old enough to be out of school, and sat down in the chair he had been offered.

'Well, Mr Graham, what can I do for you?'

'As you've probably already realised, I'm an Australian and I run a sheep station in New South Wales. My only child, Fiona, was a qualified physiotherapist and wanted to come over to this country for an extended visit to work, although God alone knows why. I happened to see in a magazine that a cove I used to know during the war had opened a number of private health clinics over here and I wrote to him as I didn't want her coming over here without anything being fixed up. He agreed to take her on and she went to work in one of his places. She was there for about a year and then a month ago she was found dead in the open-air swimming pool at this place Croxley Hall.'

'There must have been an inquest.'

'There was and the verdict was accidental death by drowning.'

'And you're not satisfied with it.'

'You're darned right I'm not. Now, look, I know just what you're thinking — another of those fathers with obsessions about their daughters — but you'd be wrong. It's true that I knew Fiona a lot better than most fathers know their daughters and, for Christ's sake, I ought to have; Annie died when Fiona was born and I brought her up on my own, that's why I'm quite sure that she would never have gone for a midnight swim in the nude.'

'Hang on a moment, you're losing me.'

'I'm sorry. The superintendent physiotherapist at that place goes for a run every morning with her dog. She found Fiona lying face-down in the pool and her clothes were folded neatly on the diving board. Fiona was a bit of a dare-devil and quite fearless on horseback, but she was terrified of water. She had a thing about it ever since the age of twelve when she very nearly drowned in the creek and she would never have gone near a swimming pool, let alone in the middle of the bloody night. And another thing, if she had taken off all her clothes to go for a swim, she'd never have folded them up neatly, she'd have thrown them on to the ground and plunged straight in.' The Australian looked away for a moment. 'She was the most God-damned untidy girl who ever lived.'

'And you'd like us to look into it further?'

'I was hoping that you might. All Fiona's belongings were packed up in a store room at the Health Farm and I came across the things she had been wearing that night — I've got them in here,' he said, making a gesture towards the hold-all.

'How can you be sure that they're the right ones?'

'Because they hadn't been laundered and I'm not a complete idiot. I don't think that a proper post mortem was done on Fiona; I mean they didn't even bother to examine her clothes and if a girl of her age is found both dead and naked, what's the first conclusion you'd come to?'

'What sort of a person was Fiona?'

'Something of a handful. It could be

that a lot of it was my fault; I was busy on the station, there wasn't much place for pretty clothes and nice manners and she was always on horseback, helping out in one way or another. When she went to do her physiotherapy training in Sydney, she suddenly discovered that there was more to life than being a tomboy and she went a bit wild — you know, with the blokes. That was the main reason I wrote to this health farm fellow — I was worried about what she might get up to in a strange country — and I thought that he might keep a watchful eye on her. Looking back on it, I think it was a mistake.'

'Why?'

'Well, as a start, I had no right to involve him in that way; I hadn't seen or heard anything of him in more than forty years and people change a lot in that time.'

'But you were close to him in the war?'

Graham's lips tightened. 'Not exactly close, but we were in the army together.'

'Have you seen him on your visit here?'

'Only very briefly. I just wanted to make it clear that I in no way held him responsible for what happened and perhaps it's not so surprising that after all those years we should have found that we had nothing left in common.'

'I take it that Fiona hasn't been buried yet.'

'No, and I suppose you're going to tell me to get on with the arrangements and then go back to Australia and forget all about it.'

Graham looked aggressively at the detective across the desk, waiting for the merest hint of a patronising smile to cross the man's face so that he could give vent to his feelings of frustration and anger.

'On the contrary, what you've told me is very concerning. As a start, I propose to get a full report on the inquest, ask one of our expert forensic pathologists to take a look at those clothes and then I suggest that we meet again, say in a week's time.'

'I wouldn't want you stirring up trouble at Croxley Hall — that wouldn't be fair on that bloke I was telling you about.'

Graham fully realised that he was trying to have it both ways and that the detective would have had every justification for saying so, but he didn't, merely nodding.

'I can understand that; what I'd suggest is that we defer a final decision about that just now and in the meantime, you have no need to worry, we won't go near it.'

'Fair enough.'

Roger Newton turned to his assistant. 'Have you any questions, Jane?'

'Do you happen to have a photograph of Fiona on you, Mr Graham?' she asked.

The man reached into the inside pocket of his jacket and took out his wallet, handing over the picture.

'May I keep it for a day or two?'

'Provided that you don't lose it — it's one of my favourites of her.'

The Australian had been fully expecting to be met with hostility, or at the very least bland reassurances, and had carefully rehearsed a tirade about the state of the country, the increasing violence in the streets and the shortcomings of the police, but now he felt that the wind had been completely taken out of his sails. The detective was too smooth by half, but he hadn't been able to take exception to a single thing the man had said. He left Scotland Yard feeling flat and humiliated, knowing that he had behaved badly. With Fiona gone, there was nothing to look forward to; it might have been tolerable if there had been someone with whom to share his grief, but as it was . . . He stood on the edge of the pavement and watched the bus approaching; he might almost as well . . .

★ ★ ★

'Well,' said Newton, 'what did you make of him?'

'One very angry Aussie who doesn't like Poms much.'

'That's true enough, but is he on to something?'

'Even if he is, I reckon it's going to be very difficult to prove at this stage. Do you think the forensic people will be able to learn anything from those clothes?'

'You don't know Golding, do you?'

'Only from the lectures he gave us.'

Newton laughed when he saw the

expression on her face. 'He may not be everyone's cup of tea, but if anyone can dig up a clue from those clothes it'll be him. He may also prove to be our trump card in dealing with our friend Graham if Fiona did die accidentally — I have a feeling that those two would be just about a match for each other and if I were to set up a little meeting . . . '

'What would you like me to do?'

'In the normal course of events, I would have suggested that you came along to the pathologist with me, but Golding being Golding, I'm not sure that that would be very wise. Why don't you see what you can dig up on this place Croxley Hall — it'll be good practice for you.'

Jane wasn't in the best of moods when she went down to the canteen for a cup of tea ten minutes later. Newton had arranged to meet her at the end of the week and how the hell, she thought, was she going to spend four days in looking into a health farm when she wasn't even allowed to visit it? The shining hour wasn't exactly improved, either, by Karen

Jackson, who joined her at one of the tables.

'Why so glum?' she asked. 'No, don't tell me — you've still got nothing to do.'

'If you must know, I've been put on to looking into a health farm where a girl was found dead under suspicious circumstances.'

'Big deal!'

'Well, at least it's something entirely on my own.'

'I thought that Svengali was never going to let you out of his sight.'

'You're just jealous, Karen, that's your trouble.'

'Jealous! I wouldn't swap places with you for all the tea in China; we all know why the big bad boss wanted you to work for him.'

'And what's that supposed to mean?'

'Oh, come on; you're not that simple. One of the blokes was telling me that he's the dirty old man to end all dirty old . . .'

'Mind if I join you ladies?'

The very large man, the button on the front of whose jacket was threatening to fly off at any moment, didn't wait for an answer and sat down next to Jane, put his cup of tea on the table and surveyed the formidable looking rock cake with every appearance of pleasurable anticipation. Karen Jackson gave her friend a look and got up to go, but when Jane went to follow, she found her way blocked by fourteen and a half stone of bone and muscle.

'I won't keep you a moment,' the man said, making a gesture towards her chair with one enormous hand. 'You're new here, aren't you?'

'Yes.'

'And you're working for Inspector Newton?'

'That's right.'

'Well, I couldn't help hearing what your friend was saying and I just wanted to tell you that it isn't true. Inspector Newton's a family man and a nicer person you couldn't hope to meet. He may have had a University education, but there's no side to him and you won't always have the good fortune to be with someone like him. I hope you make the most of it.' The man got up from his chair to make room for her to get out. 'Good luck.'

Jane was still feeling distinctly shaken when she joined Karen at the exit to the canteen.

'What did he want? As if I didn't know — it must be nice to know that the macho types are attracted to you as well as the smoothies, even if they are overweight and distinctly long in the tooth.'

'Who is he?'

'Don't you know anything that goes on around here? That was Sergeant George Wainwright, Newton's side-kick. I don't suppose he's all that bad, provided your particular kink is having it away with a gorilla.'

'Can't you ever give it a rest?'

'My, my, we have gone proper all of a sudden — sorry I spoke.'

Karen Jackson flounced off, leaving Jane staring after her; it was true, she thought, that her friend had done a good deal to liven things up during their training but, by now, the same old jokes were beginning to become more than a bit stale.

Jane wasn't feeling much brighter by

the time she got back to the office she was sharing with Roger Newton's secretary. She supposed that she ought to have been grateful for having been given a desk of her own, but the constant chatter of the typewriter was hardly conducive to concentration and try though she did, she was quite unable to think up a way of even getting hold of a brochure in the time available, short of ringing up the health farm and asking for one to be put in the first-class post. And even that would presumably breach the agreement they had made with Graham not to make direct contact with the health clinic. She shook her head and let out a loud sigh.

'That sounds bad.'

Jane glanced up to see Roger Newton's secretary looking at her, an amused expression on her face.

'I need some information and I can't think of a way of getting it.'

'I always use the Yellow Pages.'

Hah, hah, thought Jane — very funny. Nevertheless, when the woman had left the room, she had a quick look at the section entitled Health Clubs and Centres and there, staring her in the face was a large advertisement.

GLOVER'S HEALTH CLUBS

MASSAGE, HYDROTHERAPY, SAUNAS, SOLARIA.

BLOOMSBURY, HOLLAND PARK, CHELSEA.

RESIDENTIAL CENTRE, CROXLEY HALL, GLOUCESTERSHIRE.

Beneath was a telephone number and a few minutes later she had the address of the one in Chelsea.

Jane studied the brochure over a sandwich and a yoghourt at a snack-bar a few hundred yards up the road from the centre; Croxley Hall looked impressive enough from the glossy pictures, but what made her gulp were the prices, which for one week were comfortably in excess of what she earned in a couple of months. What to do next? What she really needed to do was to talk to someone who had actually spent a couple of weeks at the Clinic during the time that Fiona had been working there. But how to find that someone? What about her Uncle Henry? Her mother's brother did some dreary work in the Civil Service, but he was far from dreary himself; he had been the one to support and encourage her when she had decided to join the Metropolitan Police and surely there must be someone in his dusty club who had been to Croxley Hall, or who would at least know someone who had.

Jane was far from encouraged by the response to her phone call. Her uncle hardly seemed to be listening when she tried to explain what she wanted and that time wasn't on her side.

'I'm afraid that I can't discuss it just now,' he said. 'Hang on a moment and I'll just have a look in my diary.' He came back on the line almost at once. 'By the end of the week, you said? Look, I'm a bit tied up tomorrow and the day after and this evening, I was . . . No, that would be all right, how about my club at seven o'clock this evening?'

'I wouldn't want to . . .'

'See you there.'

Jane was left with the distinctly uncomfortable feeling that he had altered his evening arrangements just for her and it wasn't even as if it was anything really important. She took the photo that Graham had given her out of the folder and studied it carefully. The girl with the short, dark hair and who was wearing jeans and a check shirt was standing by the side of a horse smiling at the camera. What was she talking about? Of course the case was important and even if her part in it was a small one, she was going to do it to the very best of her ability.

Jane had only been to her uncle's club once before, but even so the rubicund and cheerful porter at the desk in the lobby recognised her, or, she thought, more likely put on a convincing show of pretending to do so.

'Good evening, Miss Warwick,' he said, as she rather tentatively mounted the steps, not being absolutely certain that she had got the entrance right — there was nothing so vulgar as a name-plate by the door. 'Sir Henry is waiting for you at the top of the stairs.'

It had been obvious to Jane for as long as she could remember that almost everyone was terrified of her Uncle Henry and it wasn't difficult to see why. A man in his middle fifties of only medium height and build, he had a habit of listening to what people had to say with immense concentration, his eyes unblinking behind the thick lenses of his glasses, without saying a word until they had finished and then leaving a long gap before replying.

Jane, though, didn't find him in the least daunting; she could remember cuddling up to him in front of the open fire while he read her Brer Rabbit stories, building elaborate sand castles with him on the beach in North Cornwall and visits in London to such exciting places as the London Dungeon, of which her father, a singularly strait-laced parson, wouldn't have approved at all. No, she wasn't at all frightened of him, indeed she felt rather sorry for him. He was unmarried and she had often wondered if he was a homosexual but, if so, she felt quite sure that it would be as strictly under control as everything else in his life.

Without ceremony, he ushered her straight into the dining-room, waited until they had ordered their meal and then looked at her across the table.

'I have been able to find a customer for you from that health farm of yours. Wasn't all that difficult, second man I tried, in fact — barrister by the name of Forbes-Hassett. I told him that you were thinking of working there — that do? I couldn't face him over dinner, but I've asked him to take a glass of port with us after. It'll turn out to be several, mark my words, and if ever there was an advertisement for the utter futility of regular visits to health farms, he's it. Now, tell me more about this case of yours.'

Jane did so, trying to remember every detail that Graham had given her.

'Of course the man's absolutely shattered by it all, but he was at pains to point out that he hadn't merely got a bee in his bonnet about it and I believed him. It is also obvious that her death wasn't investigated properly; it seems quite incredible to me that no one should have examined those clothes, but then I suppose that nobody suspected that her death was due to other than natural causes. There was one other thing; Graham never actually mentioned the owner of the place by name, but whenever the subject came up, I detected a distinct cooling of the atmosphere. That happened on several occasions and particularly when the war was mentioned; you don't happen to know anyone in the War Office I might ask about him, do you? His name is Glover.'

There was the usual long pause. 'Glover? How did you find that out?'

'I looked in the Yellow Pages — he owns a number of health clubs in London as well as Croxley Hall.'

Her uncle took out his diary and made a note in it. 'I'll have to see what I can do about that.' There was an even longer pause while he looked her up and down. 'I'm not sure it was wise of me to have asked you out to dinner like this.'

'I promise not to be a nuisance in the future, but it is my first proper case.'

'I assure you that it wasn't that that was concerning me, my dear, it's your weight. If you hadn't already told me that a visit there was impossible for the time being, I would have said that the best way for you to have investigated that health farm would have been to spend a couple of weeks living on fresh air and Malvern water.'

Jane smiled ruefully and eyed the boeuf bourgignon in front of her. 'It's not that I don't try, but there are so many temptations.'

'How much do you weigh? Eleven stone?'

'Have a heart — ten and a half.'

'Hmm. I'm warning you, Jane, I won't invite you out to a meal again until you're under nine stone and I hope that the sight of Forbes-Hassett will serve as a warning to you. Now, how about another spoonful of those delicious looking courgettes?'

The barrister was every bit as gross as her uncle had suggested. He was not only the fattest, but also the ugliest man that Jane had ever seen, accentuated by his black coat, the collar of which was dusted with a fine coating of scurf and his sponge-bag trousers, which, massive though they were, failed to contain his formidable paunch.

'Splendid place, Croxley Hall,' he said, nodding his head, which set his jowl shaking, 'best cuisine in the West Country.'

'In my ignorance I rather assumed that the object of places like that was to trim off some of the blubber.'

'Only for those who are masochistically inclined, my dear fellow. My particular kick is gained from being pummelled by attractive physiotherapists.' He smiled at Jane, his eyes disappearing from view as he did so. 'You must let me know when you start working there.'

'Did you happen to come across a girl called Fiona Graham during one of your visits?'

'Did I not.' His face took on a dreamy look. 'Everyone's favourite from Down Under. Sad about her — generous girl.'

'How do you mean?'

'Always prepared to leave the odd button undone to please the customers and not averse to a bit of horse-play. It's perhaps not surprising that one or two of those girls kicked over the traces from time to time, particularly with that wardress of a superintendent physiotherapist watching over them the whole time. You'll have to look out for yourself where she's concerned, my dear, she's the type who eats young fillies for breakfast.'

The man guffawed loudly, drained his glass of port and in a smooth continuous movement reached out for the decanter.

'Kicked over the traces, you said? In what way?'

'Well, there was not only Fiona going for nude bathes, but one of the others got put inside for having cocaine in her room.' He began to chuckle as he saw Jane's expression and then went into a paroxysm of coughing, having to resort to an enormous spotted silk handkerchief to wipe his streaming eyes. 'One of the OT girls by the name of Ruth, it was. Redhead, looked as if she might be a bit of a goer, but was, in fact, as quiet as a church mouse. I wasn't there when it happened, but one of the other girls told me about it when I went there on a subsequent visit.'

'When did all that happen?'

'Must have been some time last autumn. For some reason or other, her case was heard in London, or it would be more accurate to say that it would have been had the silly girl not pleaded guilty. She also had the bad luck to come up against that pompous ass Duckworth — he enjoys seeing people cringe and if she'd burst into floods of tears and promised never to do it again, he'd probably have just given her a right rolicking and let her off with a fine. As it was, when he asked her if she had anything to say, she told him that she reckoned that what she did in private was her own affair and all that that achieved was three months in Holloway. I tell you this, if I'd been defending her in front of a jury, I lay you two to one I'd have got her off; I know how to provoke that sanctimonious bugger and given the right twelve good people and true . . . '

'How was she found out?'

'Shopped, I reckon. Perhaps she turned someone down; Croxley Hall doesn't encourage 'em, but the odd individual from the pop scene manages to insinuate themself . . . and you know what they're like.'

'Does a lot of drug taking go on there?'

The barrister let out another of his loud guffaws. 'Good Lord, no. The place reeks of sanctity, not pot. That's one of its quaint attractions; do you know, each and every Sunday, they . . . '

In the next half hour, Jane was given a detailed run-down on the staff and facilities at Croxley Hall. It sounded to her like a cross between a religious retreat and a very superior massage parlour, with the senior staff strict and puritanical and the physio and occupational therapy staff quite prepared to indulge in suggestive chat and, if the barrister was to be believed, rather more than that at times.

'If you ask me,' the man said, just having looked at the empty decanter and then at her uncle with an expression of which any actor playing Oliver Twist would have been proud, but which was met with stony indifference, 'the person who really makes that place tick is Patricia Pennington. She's the Director's secretary and if they had any sense they'd beg her to take over from the senile fool who's just retired — all he ever did was wander about being agreeable, while she did all the real work. Nothing's too much trouble to her; she knows everyone who's ever been there before, takes an interest in each client personally, makes sure that important people aren't pressured by bores or social climbers and deals with the rare complaints with tact and efficiency. Only trouble with her is that she has no ambition, she isn't even in for the job.'

'So, it hasn't been filled yet?'

'It hadn't been when I was last there. If you ask me, they'll appoint an outsider — the three local candidates aren't up to much. There's Galton, who's a shade too interested in her young charges, Leggett, who's nothing but a busybody and Milroy, the estate manager, who's not only a lazy bugger, but has the millstone around his neck of a wife who's a lush.'

At that point, her uncle raised one eyebrow and when Jane nodded, he got to his feet.

'Well, my dear fellow,' her uncle said, 'some of us have to start work before lunch and we mustn't keep young Jane here out of her bed for too long.'

The barrister licked his fleshy lips, making it only too clear that he wouldn't have been averse to sharing it.

'Hope you get that job. I'll look forward to a special massage when next I'm there.'

He wiped the sweat from his forehead with his handkerchief and then bent to kiss the back of her hand. Jane had never had the experience of feeling a snail crawling over her skin, but had little doubt that it would have felt very similar and she was hard pressed not to grimace with distaste.

'Sorry about that,' her uncle said when they were standing on the steps of the club a few minutes later, 'but he was the best I could do at short notice and I did warn you.'

'Don't worry, he was perfect.'

His lips twitched momentarily. 'I'll see what I can unearth on this fellow Glover, all right?'

'That would be wonderful; thank you so much for taking all this trouble.'

'Think nothing of it.'

# 3

Jane had never been to the records' department on her own and to say that she was impressed would have been a major understatement. Within five minutes of her arrival, she was presented with a folder and was looking at a photograph of Ruth Lavington. The standard harsh, clinical full-face and profile views were hardly flattering, but she was a pleasant enough looking young woman with striking, shoulder-length red hair, but far more interesting than that was the fact that the drugs' squad had been tipped off by means of an anonymous letter. There was a photocopy of it in the file and it had been laboriously put together with pieces cut out of daily papers. Jane read it through several times.

'Drugs on a health farm? Difficult to believe, isn't it, but why not take a look in the suitcase on top of the wardrobe in the room of Ruth Lavington, one of the occupational therapists?'

The author had even been able to find the name Lavington, which looked as if it had been taken out of a telephone directory. The information had been acted upon, cocaine had been found in the place suggested and, after initially electing to go for trial by jury, the young woman in the event pleaded guilty. Jane looked at the dates and saw that the young woman had been released ten weeks earlier. What to do next? There were still three days before she was due to meet Roger Newton and so why shouldn't she see if she could trace Ruth Lavington?

The address of the young woman's next of kin, her mother, was in the records, but Holloway was the obvious place to start and she had always wanted to see inside it. Getting permission to make the visit was the least of her problems — a phone call to one of the deputy governors was enough to do the trick — but once there, she found it extremely hard going. Everyone said the same thing and that was that Ruth

Lavington had been no trouble. Despite very much keeping herself to herself, she had been pleasant to both the other prisoners and the staff alike, had rejected offers of help when she had left and earned the maximum amount of remission. Even the two inmates who had been the most friendly with her had nothing to add. Admittedly the two women were suspicious of her motives, but even making allowances for that, it seemed clear that Ruth had said almost nothing to them about her personal life, or her hopes for the future.

By the time she had finished interviewing the two prisoners, Jane was near to giving up and more as an after-thought than for any other reason, she decided to take a look at the art room, where Ruth had evidently spent a lot of her time. It would have been difficult to put into words why she knew that the woman in charge was hiding something — it wasn't true that she was deliberately obstructive — but she was quite sure, none the less.

'Look,' Jane said, after yet another question had been parried, 'we're not trying to hound Ruth, it's just that there has been an unexplained death at the clinic where she used to work and we think that the best way of making progress is to have a chat with her.'

'Why didn't you talk to her when she was here?'

'The member of staff only died less than a month ago.'

The woman looked at Jane for a moment and then seemed to make up her mind. 'I'm sorry,' she said, 'but it's not often that we get someone like Ruth here. It may have been partly because she never complained and was so helpful, particularly here in the art classes, but a number of us thought it was a disgrace that she was in prison at all and I, for one, believe that she ought to be left in peace now, if that's what she wants.'

'I do see that, but it's not now just a question of a comparatively minor offence like drug taking; we have some evidence that one of the physiotherapists there, who at first was thought to have drowned accidentally, was in fact murdered.'

Jane was fully aware that she was

stretching the truth, but she couldn't think of any other way of getting the woman's cooperation and even then, for the next half hour she was forced to admire the collection of indifferent paintings, drawings and drunken looking pieces of pottery, which were obviously her pride and joy.

'Do you have any of Ruth's work here?'

'She mostly did drawings of the other girls and they were so good that they kept them, but I do have one or two of her sketches.'

They were of a ballet dancer and had an economy of line, an animation and a lightness that made all the others look dead, flat and heavy.

'She's certainly got real talent. Why didn't she have any visitors?'

'It wouldn't be true to say that she didn't have any. She had two; one was a nice woman from the place where she worked, who came fairly soon after Ruth was sent here and then there was the second, which was the one occasion on which I ever saw Ruth really upset. Perhaps that was the reason why she refused to see anyone else afterwards.'

'Who was it?'

'Her young sister. She was the only member of the family that Ruth really cared for and she told me that it was extremely brave of her to have come. She's only fourteen and her mother expressly ordered her to have nothing to do with her sister, yet she managed to come up all the way from Brighton on her own. Ruth couldn't think how she had managed to get hold of the money or take a day off school without her mother knowing — evidently Mrs Lavington will hardly let her out of her sight. Ruth hated her mother and was determined to get her sister away one day.'

'Do you know what Ruth is doing now?'

'I've no idea. When she walked out of here three months ago, she told no one where she was going or what she was intending to do. I did ask her, but she just smiled and said she'd be OK.'

Jane left the prison both intrigued and determined to find Ruth Lavington. But how was she going to set about it? She clearly couldn't ask Patricia Pennington from Croxley Hall, who had been Ruth's visitor at Holloway and although she did have Mrs Lavington's address, a visit to her was hardly likely to be profitable as the two of them were obviously estranged. She tried hard to imagine what she would have done in Ruth's position. The fact that her career would be in ruins, that she was unlikely to have any money saved — Croxley Hall was her first appointment — and that her mother was unsympathetic, would have made it extraordinarily difficult. Would she have stayed with a friend and tried to get a job? What openings would there be for an occupational therapist who was only twenty-two and would surely be unacceptable to any respectable establishment such as Croxley Hall, or a hospital in the health service?

It took Jane quite some time to think of a way of approaching Mrs Lavington. It would be only too easy for the woman to hang up if she telephoned and that meant a visit to Brighton, but would the woman be prepared to speak to her if she did go down there? What Jane had decided to say sounded reasonable enough to her when she rehearsed it in front of the mirror, but would it be the same face to face with a woman who would almost certainly be antagonistic to her?

Jane's heart was thumping with nervous anticipation as she walked up the path and the anticlimax, when she found the semi-detached house empty, was quite devastating. She had just walked back along the garden path having had no response to her repeated rings, when an elderly woman came out of the front door of the neighbouring house, wearing rubber gloves and carrying a trowel and a pair of secateurs.

'If you're looking for Mrs Lavington,' she said, giving Jane a pleasant smile, 'she's running her dancing class; she's always there at this time on Wednesday afternoons.'

'Do you know when she's likely to be back?'

'It's generally about half-past six.'

'Oh dear, I can't really afford to wait that long. Perhaps I should go round to her class — is it far?'

'No, she holds it in St Martin's Church Hall, which is about ten minutes walk away. I hope you don't mind me asking, my dear, but you don't know Mrs Lavington very well, do you?'

'No, I've never met her. I did my training with Ruth and came across her name in an old address book; I'm working in Brighton now and thought it would be fun to contact her again. I was hoping to find out where she had got a job; I did try telephoning, but couldn't get a reply and as I happened to be passing . . .'

Jane could see how embarrassed the woman was and gave her a bright smile.

'So you haven't heard?'

'Heard what?'

'I'm afraid that Ruth ran into a bit of trouble and I don't think you'll find that Mrs Lavington will want to talk about it.'

'I see; I'm very sorry to hear about it. Nothing serious I hope.'

'I'd like to explain, I really would, but . . .'

'Don't worry, I quite understand. It's not as if I knew Ruth all that well anyway and I wouldn't want to bother her mother. Thanks for the tip.'

If ever Jane had seen relief written all over anyone's face, it was on that woman's and she immediately decided that she would have to devise some other approach. She found the church hall without difficulty and was hanging about outside, listening to the sound of a Scottish reel and trying to summon up the courage to go in, when the arrival of an elderly man wearing a dark blue blazer and tan slacks gave her the opportunity she was looking for.

'Come to collect one of the little horrors?' he asked, brushing one side of his ginger moustache with the back of his hand.

'That's right.'

'This your first time?' Jane nodded. 'Why not come in. It's worth a guinea a minute — that's why I always arrive early.'

'Won't Mrs Lavington mind?'

'Intensely, but that's half the fun. I can't stand the woman — never did like bullies. You should see the way she treats that daughter of hers.' He suddenly put his hand to his mouth in a theatrical gesture of dismay. 'You're not her favourite niece just back from Australia, are you?'

Once reassured, the man began to chuckle, opened the door and showed her to one of the chairs lining the walls with an elaborate show of courtesy. The pale complexioned woman, wearing a kilt and with her grey hair parted at one side and neatly held in place with a slide, interrupted the step she was demonstrating and gave an audible sigh.

'Don't worry about me, Mrs L.'

'Do you have to come quite so early, Major?'

'Like to see how me grand-daughter's gettin' on, don't yer know.'

The woman turned away with a slight shake of her head. Not only was she very trim, Jane thought, but in remarkable physical condition, despite the fact that she couldn't have been a day under fifty. She was constantly correcting and cajoling the girls in her class, keeping an iron grip on the group and reducing several of the less-robust members to tears, and then did a sword dance herself, showing no signs of fatigue or breathlessness.

'As you clearly seem to think that Pauline's efforts are a joke, Mary, perhaps you'd care to show us how it should really be done,' she said at the end of the next dance.

The dumpy girl at the end of the line blinked a few times behind her thick glasses and slowly came to the front of the class. If it hadn't been so cruel, it would have been like a comedy sketch; the girl, her white shirt discoloured by large damp patches under her arms, had very little idea of timing and even less grace and yet she was made to complete the whole dance, her lumpy adolescent body flopping about uncontrollably. That hadn't been the only time that Mrs Lavington had got at her either. 'Do at least pretend that you're trying, Mary; you're not meant to be treading on the swords, you know; can't you make some attempt to keep to the beat?' Those were some of the remarks that were directed at her.

'Who is that wretched girl?' Jane whispered to the man beside her after Mrs Lavington had delivered yet another broadside at her.

'You clearly haven't been here before,' he replied, 'she's Mrs L's daughter.'

'Her what?'

'Her daughter — adopted, as you might guess from looking at them together. You could say that the woman hasn't had much luck, what with Ruth as well as Mary, but on the other hand, you would equally well say that she doesn't deserve any.'

'What about her husband?'

'Died five years ago, which was the first sensible thing the poor fellow ever did.'

'Really, Major.'

'Sorry, Mrs L.'

He gave the woman a courtly bow and when she had turned away, winked and smiled broadly at Jane.

Before long, parents, grandparents, sisters and other assorted relatives began to arrive to collect the children and Jane took the opportunity to make herself scarce. She was standing in a phone-box on the other side of the road when eventually Mrs Lavington came out and she watched as the woman strode purposefully in the direction of her house, the ungainly Mary struggling to keep up a few paces behind.

Jane had already long since abandoned her second plan of pretending to be a social worker and seeing what she could get out of Mrs Lavington that way. She had a feeling, amounting to a certainty, that those pale blue eyes would see through the deception straight away. No, Mary would be the one with whom she would have the best chance, but how to get her on her own? School would obviously be the easiest place, but time was running out and in any case an approach there would be very likely to frighten her.

Jane's chance came when she was least expecting it. She had been watching the house for nearly an hour and had almost decided to wait until the girl left for school the following morning, when Mary came out of the house with a King Charles spaniel and began to make her way towards the seafront.

'You're Mary, aren't you?'

The girl, who had been leaning against the railings on the promenade and looking out to sea, whirled round and stared at Jane through her thick spectacles.

'I saw you at the church hall,' she said accusingly. 'What do you want?'

'I must speak to Ruth — urgently.'

'Why? Who are you?'

'I was in Holloway with her — that's how I know who you are. I saw you when you came to visit.'

'I don't know where she is.'

The girl was lying, Jane was sure of it. 'If you're worried about giving her address away,' she said, 'you needn't be — her telephone number would be enough.' Mary Lavington shook her head and although she hated herself for it, Jane decided that she had no alternative but to exert some pressure on her. 'I could always speak to your mother and . . . '

'Don't do that.' It was as if the words had been dragged out from the very centre of her and a tear began to run slowly down her cheek from beneath her glasses. 'I did promise Ruth I'd . . . '

'Ruth need never know that you told me and I won't say anything to your mother if . . . '

The girl gave her the number, looked at her intently for a moment as if trying to etch her face in her memory, and then went off in a travesty of a run, the dog chasing after her.

When Jane got back to the Yard, she found that the telephone number was registered in the name of a J.R. Caldwell at an address in St John's Wood and when she got there in her car at eight o'clock the following morning, she immediately wondered if Mary had been more determined than she had thought and had given her a false number. The block of flats, which was within sight of Lord's cricket ground, was practically new and with its uniformed doorman, expensively carpeted foyer and aura of luxury, was hardly the place that a jobless girl just out of prison would have been expected to be occupying.

Jane could think of no reasonable

alternative to going up to the flat on some pretext or other, but a few minutes after eight o'clock seemed much too early for any of the reasons she could think of and she decided to wait until nine, passing the time by listening to her car radio. Half an hour or so later, she was idly looking out of the window and glancing with envy at the grey suede boots and matching skirt and jacket of the young woman who was coming down the steps of the building, when, with a sudden sense of shock, she realised that it was Ruth Lavington. Jane took a quick look at the photograph on the front seat beside her; the young woman had lost weight, but that mass of red hair was unmistakable.

Jane was so intrigued by Ruth's obvious affluence — she got into a practically new Volkswagen Polo — that she decided to follow her. The journey was a short one, and less than ten minutes later the car drew up outside a building in Maida Vale, Ruth got out and, after putting some coins in the meter, ran up the steps and in through the entrance. Jane waited for a quarter of an hour and then crossed the road herself, strolling past the door. The name 'Electra Studios' on the plate at the side of the entrance conveyed nothing to her at all, but, she wondered, did the fact that the woman had used a four-hour parking meter mean that she would be driving back to her flat for lunch? It seemed worth taking a gamble on it and if she was, it gave Jane an idea about getting some more information about the ex-occupational therapist.

Jane spent the morning in her car writing up a detailed report and keeping an eye on the building, while speculating on the possible reasons for Ruth's sudden wealth. The most obvious explanation was that she was on the game, but if that was the case, how had she managed to establish herself so quickly and what about the studio? Blue films, or posing for way-out pictures perhaps? Had she got a rich lover? None of the things she could think of seemed exactly credible and she decided to wait to see what the lunch hour might bring.

Not long after noon, picking a moment

when there was no one about, Jane bent down by the Volkswagen's nearside rear wheel, pretending to inspect the heel of her shoe, then unscrewed the dust-cap and loosened the valve with her eyebrow tweezers. When she straightened up, there was still no one near and she walked fifty yards up the road and began to inspect the window display in a newsagent's shop at the corner. At a minute or two past one, just when Jane was beginning to wonder if she had guessed wrong, the young woman came out of the building and got into her car. Immediately, Jane began to walk briskly towards it and was alongside when the engine burst into life.

'Excuse me,' she said through the open window, 'but I'm afraid you've got a flat tyre.'

The young woman switched off, got out and looked down at the wheel.

'Damn and blast it — there goes my lunch hour.'

'Would you like me to change it for you? It's not as if I'm wearing anything that matters.'

'Don't worry, thanks. One of the

fellows at the studio will do it for me.'

'No problem.'

Before the other woman could say anything further, Jane had the keys out of the ignition switch, the rear door open and the spare wheel out on the pavement. She liked mucking about with cars, had done an MT course as part of her training and none of the bolts on the Volkswagen's wheel were really stiff or rusted in. In rather less than five minutes, she was tightening up the last nut, then let down the jack, returned it to its place under the floor covering at the back and finally examined the tyre.

'I can't see a hole anywhere; it may be just the valve — they sometimes come loose. It would probably be worth asking the garage to do a check on that first.'

Jane lifted the wheel up, put it into the back of the car and closed the rear door with a solid thump. She had been working as fast as she possibly could and when she wiped the sweat off her forehead with one filthy hand, she left a long streak of oily dirt. Ruth Lavington had made no attempt to help and was standing on the pavement looking at her with a mixture of awe, astonishment and, Jane thought, a certain wariness.

'After all that,' the young woman said, 'thank you seems a ridiculously inadequate thing to say.'

'That's OK.'

'Hang on a second,' she said as Jane began to walk away. 'I can't possibly leave you like that — your hands and face are in a frightful mess. Look, I live only a couple of miles or so up the road; why not come with me and have a shower and a bite to eat?'

'I wouldn't want to put you to all that trouble.'

'It's the least I can do.'

'It's very kind of you.'

'Kind of me!' Ruth Lavington shook her head. 'Come on — hop in. I'm afraid that I have to be back here by two-fifteen, but that should give us enough time. Where would you like me to drop you on the way back?'

'Warwick Avenue tube station would suit me best, but if that's out of your way . . .'

'No, of course it isn't. Where on earth did you learn to change a wheel like that? I'm ashamed to say that I wouldn't have had the least idea what to do.'

'I was in the army for a couple of years.'

There were times when Jane felt that she had developed a distinctly unhealthy talent for lying, but it was a skill that was certainly coming in useful and she could see that her explanation had been accepted without question.

'Soup, fruit and yoghourt suit you? That's what I generally have and today there isn't time for anything more elaborate.'

'That would suit me fine, thanks.'

'Why not take a shower while I get it ready? Bedroom's through there and the bathroom beyond — you'll find a clean towel in the airing cupboard in the corridor.'

The whole flat was quite something, Jane thought. However impractical, a thick-pile carpet in a bathroom seemed to her to be the height of luxury and although she had heard of people using black sheets, she had never actually seen a pair before. After her shower, she couldn't resist a look inside the long, built-in wardrobe. She slid the louvred door to one side and then very nearly cried out as she saw the gorilla's head only two feet from her. The full-length suit was astonishingly life-like and behind it, she found a selection of other objects that had her shaking her head in disbelief. Jane was so preoccupied by her discovery that she was very nearly found out; there was a gentle knock on the door and she just had time to run across to it on tip-toe before it was opened.

'Lunch is ready.'

'Won't be a moment.'

# 4

As soon as he entered the office, Roger Newton could see that Eric Golding, the forensic pathologist was in a good mood.

'Ah, there you are, my dear fellow,' he said, beaming over the top of his half-moon spectacles. 'Miss Graves!'

The doubling in volume of the pathologist's already loud voice was hardly necessary, Newton thought, as Golding's long-suffering secretary was already hovering by the door.

'Yes, Dr Golding.'

'How can you expect the worthy Inspector to ease his no doubt aching feet, if you will persist in using the one spare chair as an impromptu filing cabinet.'

'But Dr Golding, you said . . . '

'Excuses, excuses, nothing but excuses. Get rid of them, woman.'

Newton took a step forward to help the secretary to lift the two-foot pile of folders.

'No, no, my dear fellow. You may not believe it, but I pay that woman good money to keep this place in order and anyway, the exercise will do her good; she needs to develop those miserable fragments of tissue she calls muscles. And Miss Graves.'

'Yes, Dr Golding.'

'Two coffees. And don't try to palm me off with that synthetic, decaffeinated muck.'

'But Dr Golding, you know what your doctor said, he warned . . . '

'Do as I ask, just this once, would you please, Miss Graves? You may not believe this, but the Inspector and I have important matters to discuss. Oh, and before you go, where is the Medical Directory?'

'It's in the bookcase, sir, just to your left.'

'So it is. What an eagle eye, you have, to be sure. Let's have it, then. Part two — Pembury, Arthur Pembury.'

Golding could easily have stretched out an arm for it himself, but instead, he sat back in his chair with a self-satisfied smile on his face as the secretary put the files down on the table, scuttled round behind him, flicked through the pages and put the open volume down on the blotter.

'The man's a fool and an incompetent fool to boot.'

'Who?'

'This fellow Pembury,' Golding said, handing the large, red-covered book across the desk. 'He's the pathologist, although I don't know how he has the nerve to call himself one, who did the autopsy on that girl Fiona Graham.'

'He seems well enough qualified.'

'Qualifications, my dear Newton, are meaningless; it's a feel for the job one needs and if that's lacking, all the letters in the world after your name, don't signify a thing. No doubt it's the same in your line of country. I digress. A singular case this, most intriguing. Now, let me get this straight; this Miss Galton was on her usual morning run and only went towards the swimming pool because her dog was making a fuss about something in that direction.'

'Yes, that's right. Straight away, she saw

the girl lying naked and face down in the water and dived in. She turned her over, pulled her to the shallow end by her hair and then managed to get her out of the water by climbing up the steps backwards and lifting her up under the arms.'

'Have you questioned Miss Galton yourself?'

'No. For the time being we don't want anyone to know that we are unhappy about the coroner's verdict, but she made a long statement at the inquest and repeated it to Fiona's father, at the same time as she handed over his daughter's personal belongings, including, of course, the unlaundered clothes she had been wearing that night and which I gave you the other day.'

'I see. Well, she next held the girl's head down over the edge of the pool to try to drain some of the water out of her air passages and then attempted cardiac massage and artificial respiration for some ten minutes before abandoning her efforts and covering the body with a tarpaulin. She then took the clothes, which had been neatly folded and placed on the spring board, back to the house and telephoned the doctor.'

'That's correct. She told Graham that the only reason she moved them at all was because her dog was sniffing around them. She left them in Fiona's room when she went in there to find the name and address of her next of kin and then forgot all about them. They were packed up with all her other belongings and left in a store room until Graham handed them over to me.'

'I'll refrain from making comments about your country colleagues, but our friend Pembury shows all the characteristics of someone who decides in advance what has happened and then, surprise, surprise, his findings fit in neatly with the theory. He considered that all the superficial injuries were caused after death by Miss Galton's efforts at pulling her out of the swimming pool and trying to revive her.'

'But that wasn't the case.'

'No. The haematoma under the scalp over the vertex of the skull was definitely inflicted before death; I won't go into details, but the characteristics of ante-and post-mortem bruising are quite different.'

'What might have been responsible for that blow on her head?'

'Something blunt — the skin wasn't split.'

'Anything else?'

The pathologist reached down and pulled out the pile of clothes from the cardboard box by the side of his chair. He put the green tracksuit and tennis shoes to one side and lifted up the white cotton pants between his index finger and thumb.

'It'll be clearer when I show you the photographs.' He took several prints out of the folder and handed one across. 'This is an enlargement of their inner surface and this is the same view taken under ultra-violet light. You can no doubt just make out the faint mark on the first exposure, but note how clearly the fluorescence shows up on the second.'

'So they're seminal stains?'

The pathologist nodded. 'I've no doubt of it. I also carried out a Florence test using potassium iodide and aqueous iodine solution and the typical crystals appeared. And that's not all.' He passed another photograph across to the detective. 'In this magnified view you will observe that there are three hairs partly buried in the material — they were situated in the region of the most dense staining and I've marked it out in coloured chalk on the gusset here.'

Newton looked at the print and then at the material, using a powerful magnifying glass.

'And?'

'Two of them are human, with the characteristic oval appearance on section, which signifies body hair, and which undoubtedly belonged to the young woman, but the third, a white one, came from a horse.'

'A horse?'

The pathologist's lips twisted into the suspicion of a smile as he saw the detective's expression. 'Yes, equus caballus of the family Equidae, the common or garden horse, but before your imagination gets too overheated, I would assure you that the stains are quite definitely human in origin — the high alkaline phosphatase content makes that certain.'

'Was there any evidence of rape?'

'There was some minor bruising in the genital region, but no more than one might see after, how shall I put it, enthusiastic intercourse with consent. The chest bruising was entirely consistent with Miss Galton's efforts at resuscitation and was definitely inflicted post-mortem.'

'What about the cause of death?'

'That was the one thing that Pembury made a thorough job of. Fiona Graham's death was definitely due to drowning; he was able to demonstrate that the water in her air passages had the same chlorine content as that in the pool. The man was so proud of that elementary piece of detective work that he completely neglected to make any enquiry about the clothes.'

'Hmm. I suppose she might have decided to cool off after whatever fun and games she had gone in for, dived in, hit her head on the bottom and then drowned after stunning herself.'

'Not a bad try, my dear Newton, and just about credible, I suppose, provided you choose to forget her fear of water and the fact that she didn't go in off the spring board. It isn't at all likely that she would have been able to hit the bottom hard enough just by going in from the side.'

'Any theories yourself?'

'Theories, my dear fellow, are your responsibility; I have quite enough to do picking up the pieces after my incompetent colleagues and having to live with that apology of a secretary of mine without that. Miss Graves!'

The woman put her head round the door and blinked uncertainly at him.

'Have you been attempting to grow a coffee bush out there, Miss Graves?'

'I'm sorry, Dr Golding, but I thought that you wouldn't want to be disturbed. You may remember that when I last came in with . . .'

'You're not paid to think, Miss Graves, you're paid to carry out and indeed anticipate my wishes. Is that too much to ask?'

Newton thought, not for the first time, that the answer to that was a very firm yes, but long experience had taught him that the seemingly long-suffering Miss Graves was all part of the plot; people felt sorry for her, got angry with Golding, which immediately put him at an advantage.

★ ★ ★

Roger Newton couldn't help reflecting on how much things had changed since he had joined the Force and even, in fact, since he had married, which was after all only ten years ago. Certainly, at that time, he wouldn't have been able to foresee himself discussing such intimate details as those that Golding had discovered on Fiona Graham's underwear with a young woman not long out of school, let alone the fact that when he did so, she showed not the slightest embarrassment.

'What do you make of it?' he asked when he had finished filling in the background details.

'I can't immediately think of any theory better than the one you put to Dr Golding, but I suppose it's just possible that she committed suicide after being raped.'

Newton thought about the suggestion for a moment or two before replying.

'That's an interesting idea, but there are several things against it; it wouldn't explain the injury to her head, she also doesn't seem to have been the sort to go in for killing herself, but more important than that, if she really did have a phobia about water, she would hardly have done it that particular way. And then again, I can't recall ever having heard of anyone stripping off like that to drown themselves. No, having had quite a long time to think about it, I believe that our Australian friend is right.'

'You mean that Fiona was murdered?'

'According to Golding that blow on her head occurred before her death; she could have been stunned and then thrown in to make it look as if she had gone for a midnight swim.'

'That still doesn't explain the horse's hair.'

'No, indeed it doesn't.'

'Nor the fact that one of the occupational therapists at Croxley Hall was given three months in Holloway recently for having cocaine in her room.'

Newton raised one eyebrow. 'Tell me more.'

He listened in silence, making some notes on the pad in front of him and then looked at her intently for a moment when she had finished.

'I realise that I was exceeding my brief, but it seemed too good an opportunity to miss.'

The detective laughed. 'My being temporarily struck dumb was because of admiration rather than for any other reason. Well done, well done indeed; you did a really excellent job, particularly in such a short time.'

Jane coloured slightly. 'I had a lot of luck, really.'

'Fiddlesticks. You make your own luck in this game and that's what you did. It's extremely interesting, too; why did that girl get such a stiff sentence?'

'I wondered about that, too. Evidently, at first she elected to go for trial in front of a jury, but then, when it came to it, she pleaded guilty and had the bad luck to come up in front of a judge with a mission to stamp out drug taking. A barrister to whom I spoke seemed to think that even then if she'd done the humble and contrite act, she might well have got off with a suspended sentence, or even a fine, but evidently she refused to say a word except to make the point that what she did in private was her business, which the judge interpreted as insolence.'

'And she didn't appeal against the sentence?'

'No and that was also something the barrister couldn't understand.'

'I see. Did you get an opportunity to check on that studio?'

'Not properly, but I did find out that Electra is a company that produces animated cartoons for advertising. Someone at Thames told me that it has an excellent reputation.'

'To have got a job in a place like that so soon and with a luxury flat thrown in suggests that she must have a powerful friend somewhere.'

'I don't think that there can be much doubt about that, unless she had money of her own, which doesn't seem very likely. There's also a boyfriend on the scene — I found a pair of large slippers under the bed and some rather unusual equipment in the wardrobe.'

'Such as?'

Jane had a sudden memory of what Karen had said about George Wainwright and was hard pressed not to giggle.

'Well, there was a gorilla suit, some leather restraints and various other accessories including, how shall I put it, some mechanical aids.'

Newton let out a great hoot of laughter. 'Horse hairs in the underwear, gorilla suits in the wardrobe — whatever next?'

'I did just wonder if Ruth was on the game, but I doubt very much if it would be possible in that block of flats, particularly as there is always a porter on duty in the lobby.'

'Curiouser and curiouser. It certainly looks as if we are going to have to pay a visit to this Croxley Hall place, however much Graham dislikes the idea. Have you got that brochure with you?'

Jane handed it across and the detective

looked through it briefly.

'Looks quite a place,' he said and was just about to give it back when something on the back page caught his eye. 'Printed for Glover Enterprises by Alan Juckes, Limited, Bristol. Good God, it can't be. Let me have *Who's Who* will you?' Newton read the entry and then leaned back in his chair. 'That very firmly puts the cat amongst the pigeons.'

'What does?'

'Glover.'

'The man who owns the health clinics?'

'How did you know that?'

'His name was in the Yellow Pages; you remember I told you that that was how I got hold of the brochure.'

'And the name of Glover didn't ring any bells?'

'No, should it have?'

'Len Glover is not only reputed to be a millionaire, but he also happens to be an MP with a bee in his bonnet about the police. A totally independent complaints' procedure, no right of entry into houses in drink and drugs' cases, control of the Met. police by the GLC; those are three of his causes and to say that we would be treading on eggshells by going down there would be a major understatement, but I don't see what else we can do.'

'Couldn't we go as clients?'

'I suppose I could try to persuade Kershaw, but I can't see him agreeing — it would cost far too much. On the other hand, Fiona's death clearly can't just be ignored.'

'What I don't understand is why Ruth Lavington's case didn't make the front page of every single tabloid.'

'Neither do I; one would have thought that it would have been the scoop of the decade. I'll clearly have to tackle Kershaw, but first I need to do some homework on that case.'

\* \* \*

Commander Kershaw put down the typewritten report on the top of his desk and began the comfortable ritual of filling his pipe.

'Regular hornets' nest you seem to be in the process of stirring up, Newton. Do you really think that this girl was murdered?'

The detective nodded. 'You know what Golding's like, he will insist on sticking to the facts and leaving the theories to us, but I did get him to agree that the most likely explanation to fit all the facts was that someone stunned her with a blow to the top of the head and then threw her into the pool while still alive, where of course she drowned.'

'And that's not the half of it, either, is it? What about this other woman, Ruth Lavington?'

'After receiving the anonymous letter, the drugs people went charging in and I gather it was only after she elected to go for trial before a jury that they discovered who ran the company that owned Croxley Hall. I haven't been able to get right to the bottom of it all, but there was a distinct hint of lots of big guns going at each other hammer and tongs behind the scenes. The chief constable and high powered solicitors were certainly involved and I can't believe that Glover wasn't sticking in his oar somewhere along the line. Accusations of evidence being planted were bandied about and hints dropped that if the case were abandoned, nothing more would be heard about it. I wonder what made Ruth plead guilty; perhaps Glover decided that the case was a bit too close to home to be worth fighting and bribed her to keep her mouth shut by the offer of a nice flat and a job. The sentence she received must have rocked them both back on their heels a bit.'

'Who was the chief constable?'

'Lucas.'

'There's your answer, then. You know how he likes to jump in with both feet and he'd have asked for nothing better than a major confrontation with Glover.'

'Our friend the MP must have done some pretty nifty footwork to have kept Fleet Street quiet.'

'There are ways, as you very well know. There might only have been a reporter from the local press at the court and he might have decided that he didn't want his legs broken, or worse.'

'You don't really believe that a man like Glover would really . . . '

Kershaw smiled. 'Just letting the old imagination run riot for a change. Incidentally, how did you manage to come up with all this — good luck, or inspiration?'

'It was nothing to do with me; I just asked Jane Warwick to look into Croxley Hall for me and she dug it all out. She went ferreting around the records' department, or something.'

'And so?'

'I think that a look around that health farm ought to be our next step.'

'And bring the wrath of Glover even more firmly down on our heads? There's not much to go on, you know.'

'We could go down there as clients; I realise it would be expensive, but it's either that, the direct approach, or giving the whole thing up.'

'We?'

'Yes. Jane Warwick would be a great asset; she would be able to sound out the physios and OT girls in a way that I couldn't.'

'I have yet to meet this paragon of yours; I take it that she speaks proper.'

'She certainly is aware of the use of adverbs and more than that, as an adolescent she had the not uncommon obsession with horses.'

'Ah, yes, the mystery of the white charger that has the habit of shedding its hairs in curious places.' Kershaw got up and walked across to the window and stood there for several minutes contemplating the scenery. 'How trustworthy is that girl of yours?' he asked without turning round.

'In what way do you mean?'

'We can't afford to have everyone down there knowing what we're up to and she is only a beginner.'

'I've been very impressed by her so far and I don't think you need have any worries on that score; in any case, I'll be there to keep an eye on her.'

'What about this fellow Graham?'

'He seemed just as anxious as us not to stir Glover up and I'm sure I can keep him quiet.'

Kershaw sighed. 'Very well, then, but two weeks is all you can have.'

'Thank you, sir.'

'What about the worthy Wainwright? You haven't finally decided to give him a rest, have you?'

'No, certainly not. He'll be our back-up man — he'll be able to put up at a pub nearby.'

'Well, I suppose that's better than trying to pass him off as a boot-boy. Do watch your step, won't you?'

'Don't worry sir, I will.'

Newton winced as Kershaw held out the folder and he went to take it with his left hand.

'What's up with you?'

Newton grinned ruefully. 'Ruined my shoulder painting the ceiling of the dining-room.'

'You poor old man. Now I know why you're so keen to go to that health farm.'

# 5

If there's one thing I'm going to do, Jane Warwick said to herself, as she stood in front of the mirror in her room at Croxley Hall, it's to lose some weight. It wasn't only her uncle who had made remarks about it; Roger Newton had also pointedly told her that the cuisine that the barrister, Forbes-Hassett, had so lovingly described, was not going to be for her and the final straw had been the expression on the doctor's face during the medical examination she had had an hour after her arrival at the health farm. He had looked at the reading on the scales and then his eyes had travelled up and down her body as she stood there in her bra and pants.

'We're going to have to do something about that,' he said, making disapproving clicking sounds with his tongue.

She was forced to admit that the man had a point; there had been recent problems in doing up the waist-band of her jeans, belts had had to be let out another hole and as she turned sideways, she could see that there was a distinctly teddy bear look to her profile. Jane hurriedly put on her dressing-gown when she heard the soft knock on the door and opened it to see a pleasant-looking woman standing outside. She looked to be in her late forties with dark hair containing a few flecks of grey and she was wearing a flowered dress, which failed to conceal the fact that her figure was, to say the least of it, comfortable.

'Hello,' the woman said, 'I'm Pat Pennington, the secretary here. I thought I'd just pop in to make sure that you were settling in all right.'

'That's very nice of you. Why not come in for a moment?' Jane pointed to the untidy pile of clothes on the bed and gave her a rueful smile. 'Excuse the mess, but I was just trying to prove to myself that the doctor's criticisms of my figure weren't justified — I failed.'

The woman let out a tinkling laugh. 'I'm hardly an advertisement for this place myself, but then I gave up the unequal struggle years ago. I see that you've booked in for a fortnight; I do hope you have a happy stay.'

'I'm sure I will — I'm looking forward to plenty of riding.'

'You've come to the right place for that. Do you manage to fit in any while you're in London?'

'Not as often as I would like; I'm too busy and too much on the move for that.'

'What do you do?'

The woman seemed genuinely interested and Jane saw no harm in giving her alter-ego a try-out. The manager of a pop group — unnamed for reasons of discretion — had seemed to her to be the easiest way of explaining why she had enough money to come to a place like Croxley Hall. She was quite sure that a woman like Pat Pennington wouldn't approve, but she couldn't have been more wrong.

'What a wonderful job!' the woman said. 'You are enterprising. I'm not surprised you need a break — it must be most exhausting.'

Pat Pennington was so easy to talk to that Jane got rather carried away and said rather more than she had intended.

'You won't tell anyone else about this, will you? People always seem to want autographs or tickets and I really do want to get right away from it all.'

'Of course you do. Don't worry and if anyone or anything bothers you while you're here, you will feel free to let me know, won't you?'

Jane was greatly reassured by the woman's visit; her stay at the health farm would be fun and she was going to lose weight, she really was. It was one thing, though, to have good intentions and loads of determination when it was only five o'clock in the afternoon and she had fortified herself with a substantial pub lunch before arriving at Croxley Hall, but quite another when she had to face the evening meal. However attractively set out, what was a salad and a glass of carrot juice compared with steak and kidney pie, a gargantuan jacket potato with a large pat of farmhouse butter in the centre and home-made apple crumble and cream?

Jane's mouth began to water at the memory of it and she looked up imploringly at the waitress who was passing her table.

'Yes, madam?'

'Is that all we get?'

'I could bring you another glass of carrot juice, if you like.'

Jane let out an audible groan, shook her head and then, to take her mind off her rumbling stomach, looked round the dining-room. In her experience, dining-rooms were normally happy places, full of conversation, conviviality and laughter, but this one was like the refectory of a silent order of monks, who were dedicated to a life of mortification of the flesh. People were glancing around furtively, deliberately trying to avoid catching each other's eye, nibbling listlessly at radishes and slices of cucumber and sipping their drinks in all too obvious misery.

Inside ten minutes, the place was all but empty and Jane began to cut up her last slice of tomato into tiny pieces, eating each morsel slowly and carefully. Just as she had speared the last fragment with her fork, she looked up to see the waitress watching her; the young woman could best have been described as homely, with glasses and untidy hair and her figure was not exactly made for the white blouse and black skirt, which hung awkwardly from her ample hips. Her lips were screwed up tightly and Jane thought for a moment that she was in pain, but then she realised what the waitress was doing and burst into a hopeless fit of the giggles herself, having to take refuge behind her napkin to avoid giving in to it completely.

When the only other occupant of the dining-room had got up to leave, the waitress came across to Jane's table.

'I'm sorry, I didn't mean to be rude, but you should have seen your expression.'

'That's all right. Is it always as bad as this?'

The young woman wiped her streaming eyes with her handkerchief. 'Well, most people manage to survive the first two or three days reasonably well, but then it really begins to get to them — that is if they're not cheating. I reckon I can always tell which ones are.'

'Have you been here long?'

'Six months, but I must say that it seems much longer. My father thought it would keep me out of mischief and at the same time get me to lose some weight before I go to University in October. I don't know about the first, but you can see that the second hasn't exactly been a wild success. Still, better plump and cheerful than thin and as miserable as sin, at least that's the way I try to comfort myself.'

'You don't have to live on this stuff, do you?'

The girl giggled. 'That's supposed to be the idea, but what do you think?'

'You must let me in on your secret some time.'

'There are compensations away from here, though; I can ride as much as I like during my time off and I have . . . ' She stopped speaking as the head waiter came into the dining-room and then bent over the table to pick up the plate. 'I'll be off at nine and I've got some home-made fruit cake in my room,' she whispered. 'Meet you by the oak tree near the tennis court.'

Jane almost danced a jig on her way back to her room, her rumbling stomach forgotten; she had been dreading the following morning and her first visit to the gym when she knew she would have to pump one of the physio or occupational therapists, but now it looked as if she had an immediate ally and one who not only sounded as if she would be good for a gossip, but who might also help to keep body and soul together. On top of that, the young woman with her plummy voice, which sounded as if it had been moulded at Cheltenham Ladies' College rather than anywhere more humble, was clearly no ordinary waitress and was obviously keen on riding, which should mean that she would have come across Fiona. It was true that Roger Newton wasn't due for another couple of days and he had told her to be particularly careful what she said and did until he arrived but, she thought, making friends with the waitress wouldn't risk anything.

A few minutes after nine, Jane strolled across the grass towards the oak tree;

there was no sign of anyone and for a moment she wondered if her good luck had deserted her and if the girl had had second thoughts, but then a figure appeared from behind it.

'Psst. It's me, Angela. My room is at the top of the tower above the main entrance — it's the only one on the third floor. Meet me there in five minutes. I'm not supposed to have visitors, so make sure you're not seen.'

Jane very nearly had another fit of the giggles, the waitress was appropriately named, it was like a scene from an Angela Brazil novel but, even so, when she opened the front door she had a distinct sinking feeling in the pit of her stomach at the thought of meeting Miss Leggett, the daunting housekeeper who had shown her to her room that afternoon. Whatever sort of excuse would she be able to make for wandering about in the area which was obviously largely used for administration? She only really began to feel secure when she had negotiated two flights of the carpeted main staircase and was on the wooden boards of the flight up to

Angela's room. The very first step on which she put her weight let out an ear-splitting creak and try as she did, the same was repeated on each succeeding one. Any minute, she was expecting someone to come out of the room on the second floor where she had seen a light under the door, but she finally made it safely to find the girl standing at the head of the stairs.

'Angela Westmoreland,' she said, extending her hand.

'Jane Warwick.'

'Super. Welcome to my humble abode.' She went inside and threw open the window. 'Not bad, is it?'

'Bags of room and what a wonderful view.'

Jane leaned out and although the light was beginning to fade, could make out the tower of the chapel nestling in the trees, the swimming pool to the right and, in the distance, extensive woods.

' 'Rapunzel, Rapunzel, let down your golden hair.' Fat chance of any dashing prince being available by the look of those ghastly people having supper.'

Angela laughed. 'Those in the other dining-room are a bit better, but not a lot and you're quite right, the lettuce leaf brigade are all appalling, that's why I couldn't believe it when I saw you. Why pay all that money to starve yourself half to death? It's not even as if you needed to slim.'

Jane patted her stomach ruefully. 'Thanks for that, but I wish it was true. I'm not paying actually, it's my employer. He's stinking rich and has issued me with an ultimatum; down by a stone and a half in the next fortnight or I'll be out on my ear. He says I'm bad for their image.'

'Crikey, that'll take some doing — I'd rather remain poor, happy and plump. Anyway, even if you are serious, the first day doesn't count.'

Jane watched in amazement as Angela drew on a pair of rubber gloves and thrust one arm up inside the large chimney, which was set on one side of the room.

'What on earth's that in aid of?'

The girl blew off the dusting of soot from the cylindrical cake tin and grinned.

'We're not allowed to keep food in our rooms and I hide it on the ledge up there out of sight of prying eyes.'

'But nobody else comes up here, do they?'

'You can't have come across Miss Leggett yet.'

'Who? The gorgon who showed me to my room this afternoon?'

'You obviously have. It was on account of her that my father found out about my secret supplies — you may find this difficult to believe, but he's a bishop and has some old-fashioned and rather directly painful ways of enforcing discipline. That wasn't the worst part, though; I also had to listen to the twenty minute version of his sermon on trust.'

'You're having me on.'

'No, really. Just take a look at him.'

Angela went across to the dressing-table and handed across the leather wallet with a colour photograph on the inside. Jane glanced at the forbidding looking man in his black suit and gaiters and quickly decided that the young woman had been telling the truth. At least, she thought, Angela's mother, who was standing by his side in full evening dress and wearing a magnificent tiara, looked at least half-human.

'Sickening pair, aren't they? Ma won't be wearing her crowning glory again, though; she had it pinched a few months ago. It was taken from the Bishop's palace while they were spending a couple of weeks here. That'll give you some idea of how dim they are; they're devotees of this place and Leggett actually impresses them. That's what gave them the idea of sending me here to work — I don't think I could have stood it if it hadn't been for Pat Pennington.'

'That nice woman who's the secretary here?'

'That's right, she's an absolute sweety. She invited me out to tea when I was homesick and we had a lovely chat. She also slips me the odd chocolate when no one is looking.'

Angela opened the cake tin, cut a generous slice and gave it to Jane on the lid.

'Watch out for crumbs, won't you?'

Jane took a large bite and nodded appreciatively. 'Mmm, just what I needed. I don't know how you have the nerve to carry on like this after what happened — I'd have been too scared if my father was like yours. How did Leggett find out about it in the first place?'

Angela giggled. 'That's quite a story. I was sharing with a right snot of a girl called Helen at the time, who was one of the other waitresses, and Leggett must have had a spare key, gone for a snoop and found my cache.'

'But couldn't Helen have told on you?'

'She might have had the idea — we hated each other's guts — and I half-suspected her, but when I was moved here, which, surprise, surprise, is right above Leggett's room — my dear father's suggestion — I got proof.'

'How?'

'I was telling Fiona, one of the physios I used to go riding with, all about it and she thought up the scheme.'

'What scheme?'

'Well, as you saw, there's a ledge up the chimney and we dislodged some soot and left it in the grate. When I came down for work that evening, I made sure that I passed Leggett on the stairs and when she saw me munching something and the soot mark on my forehead, you could almost hear the cogs enmeshing in what passes for her brain. Her face really lit up and, do you know, that was the first and last time I ever saw her smile. She wouldn't have been smiling a few minutes later, though; we'd put a really strong mouse-trap on the ledge and it caught her across the finger. She lost a nail and it served the bag right. If Nosey Parkers will go snooping around in locked bed-rooms . . .'

'What did she do about it?'

'There wasn't a thing she could do.' They both heard the loud creaking sound outside and Angela put her finger to her lips. 'Leggett!' she whispered, hastily turning the key in the lock, giving Jane the cake tin and pushing her behind the door. 'Don't make a sound.'

To the accompaniment of further sounds from outside, the girl switched on her radio, adjusted the volume and as the door knob began to turn, started to pull off her clothes.

'Angela! Angela, did I hear voices in there? Open the door at once.'

Her bra, which Jane noted with amusement was held together at the back by a safety pin, joined the rest of her clothes and she gave a wink.

'At once, Miss Leggett?'

'You heard what I said.'

The woman's gasp when she saw the naked apparition in front of her was clearly audible to Jane and she had to exert every ounce of self-control not to burst out laughing.

'Angela! What is the meaning of this?'

'I was getting ready for bed, Miss Leggett, and you did say at once.'

'Put something on — this instant.'

'You can come in if you like, Miss Leggett, I'm not shy. Did you want me for anything?'

'I merely came up to ask you to turn your radio down.'

The woman went back down the stairs to the accompaniment of another loud series of creaks and Angela fell back on the bed, laughing silently with the tears running down her cheeks.

'You should have seen her expression when I licked my lips and asked her in,' she said, when she was capable of speech, 'she looked as if she thought I was about to rape her. Mind you, I wouldn't have tried that on with Miss Galton, the boss physiotherapist; she might have taken up the invitation.'

'What on earth gave you the idea of doing that?'

'Fiona again. She told me that Leggett came across her sunbathing once in the altogether and fled a mile when she got up and went towards her. Ridiculous, isn't it? A body's a body, even when in my case, whoever was responsible forgot to say when.'

Jane shook her head. 'I'd better be going before I have a heart attack. How do you get down those stairs without making a racket?'

'On the bannisters; I've loosened all the floor boards as an early warning system. Don't bother, though, I'll take you down; the loo's on the floor below and even if

Leggett's in her room, she won't dare to come out now. Finish your cake, though; you'll need strength to see you through the next two weeks.'

'OK, thanks. You said something about riding and I also read about it in the brochure — what's it like?'

'Super. Why not come with me tomorrow? I have a couple of hours off at four and I usually go then — it'll be much more fun with two of us.'

Jane only appreciated just how lucky she had been to meet and strike up an immediate friendship with Angela when she had finished the morning session in the gym. The other people in her class had ignored her completely, except for one middle-aged, paunchy man, who kept ogling her, and the physiotherapists were either too busy or too much under the eagle eye of Miss Galton to have either the time or the inclination to chat. In any case, by lunch time, Jane was aching all over from the unaccustomed exercise, was desperately hungry and in no mood to do anything but have a large lunch and sunbathe by the pool. When the large lunch turned out to be cucumber yoghourt and a celery, nut and green pepper salad, she couldn't imagine how she was going to be able to get through the afternoon work-out, let alone face a ride as well.

'I'm sorry, Angela, I really am, but I don't think I can make it, I'm absolutely shattered already,' she said, as the waitress brought her a second glass of Malvern water with a slice of lemon in it.

'That's OK, it is a bit hot, anyway. I've got another idea — meet me behind the chapel at four-thirty.'

An anti-cyclone had been almost stationary over the British Isles for a week already and it wasn't just hot, it was baking. Angela refused to say where she was taking her and by the time they had climbed through the gap in the fence behind the kitchen garden and were skirting a field in which a couple of horses were grazing, Jane could feel the sweat trickling down under her arms and slapped her neck irritably as an insect bit her.

'Not far, now.'

At least, once they were in the wood it was a lot cooler and after another five minutes, Angela pointed to a gap in the trees.

'There it is.'

The derelict stone barn at the edge of the copse was surrounded by tall weeds and didn't look as if it had been disturbed for years.

'Hang on a minute while I make sure the coast's clear.' Angela disappeared into the barn and then came back almost at once. 'Right, give me a hand with the ladder, will you? It's in the ditch over there under those leaves.'

When they had climbed into the loft, Angela pulled the ladder up and then stood with her hands on her hips, looking at Jane with a grin on her face.

'Well, what do you think of it?'

'Very snug, but how on earth did you manage to get all this together so quickly — you've only been here such a short time.'

'It was mostly Fiona's doing.'

'Who? The physio who set that trap for the dreaded Miss Leggett?' Angela nodded. 'But won't she mind you having brought me here?'

'Haven't you heard?'

'Heard what?'

'She was drowned in the swimming pool a couple of months ago.'

'But how terrible.'

'It was. She was so full of life and the only one of that stuck-up lot in the physio department to take any notice of a poor down-trodden domestic like me. At first, it gave me a funny feeling coming here again after what happened, but I think Fiona would have wanted me to. If you ask me, she might easily have been coming back from here the night it happened. She told me she'd found a new fella she fancied and it's warm and dry up here.'

It was, too. Jane looked round and could see that the roof of the barn was obviously weather proof and the blankets, books and magazines were free from any trace of damp.

'There's some cider under the straw over there — care for a glass?'

'Thanks.'

Jane watched with mounting anguish as, after she had poured the drinks, Angela opened a tin of paté and spread it thickly on a piece of ryvita. She had been feeling guilty about having accepted the cake on the previous evening and if she really was going to lose weight . . . She shook her head resolutely as Angela held it out.

'I think I'd better give that a miss, thanks all the same. Anyway, I'm past it.'

'You do sound in a bad way.'

'I am.'

Jane stretched out on one of the blankets, put a cushion under her head and idly began to flick through the pages of one of the magazines from the top of the pile nearby.

'Crikey! These are a bit strong, aren't they?'

'Fiona told me that it was one of her blokes who liked them, not her; she always said that she preferred to do it rather than talk about it or look at pictures.'

'Who was this fellow?'

'I don't know; he either left or she gave

him the push before I came here. She wasn't the sort to let the grass grow under her feet, though, and just before she was drowned she told me that she had her eye on someone new and that it would be a challenge as she was quite sure that it was going to be the first time for him.'

'And you don't know who he was, either?'

'No. I don't.' Angela suddenly looked up. 'You're not interested, are you?'

'I might be.'

The girl giggled and then blushed. 'Fiona was always telling me that unless I got some experience in, I'd fail the practical when it came to marriage, but . . .'

'I'm surprised that no one else has found this place; it looks as if the farm hasn't been a going concern for years.'

'No, it hasn't, but I suppose that no one but Fiona thought up the idea of nicking a ladder to get up here. She did tell me, though, that . . .'

'Go on.'

'It's rather rude, I'm afraid, and I'm not sure that you wouldn't . . .'

Jane laughed. 'You can't leave it in the air like that; I'm shock-proof.'

'Well, she was up here alone one Sunday, tidying up and getting in supplies for a session with her bloke, when she heard a noise from down there. It was Ruth, one of the occupational therapists and a gorilla.'

Jane choked on her drink and went into a fit of coughing. 'A gorilla?'

'Not a real one, you loony, just some guy in a suit.'

'It must have been rather hot.'

'It wasn't mid-summer then, for goodness' sake. Anyway, Fiona told me that it was fantastically realistic and she had a grandstand view through that large crack in the floorboards over there. Evidently they mucked around for a bit and then, do you know what?' Angela picked up one of the magazines and after leafing through it, passed it across. Jane glanced at the strikingly explicit colour photograph, which was in sharp focus, and raised one eyebrow. 'They did that. Ugh — I'd never let that happen to me, I just couldn't.'

'Oh, I don't know. It's quite nice, really,

once you get used to it.'

Angela squirmed in delighted horror. 'Oh, Jane, you can't have — you're teasing.'

'Who was the gorilla? Anyone from here?'

'You're not thinking of . . . I say, you are a dark horse. I'm sorry to have to disappoint you, but Fiona either didn't know or wasn't telling.'

'What about Ruth? What did you say her other name was?'

'Lavington.' Angela giggled again. 'She won't be able to help you either — she got busted by the law for having cocaine in her room. I should think she'd have needed it to pluck up courage to do that. I say, you're not into the drugs' scene as well, are you?'

Jane smiled, she hoped enigmatically. 'Who ratted on her?'

'It all happened before I came, but Fiona told me that it must have been Leggett — that's one of the reasons she hated her so. The feeling was entirely mutual.'

'Why was that?'

'Well, a few weeks ago, Leggett was showing one of the trustees, a bloke called Miles Randell, out to his car after he had been on a tour of inspection. It was pouring with rain and when she opened the golf umbrella, which they keep in the front hall, a shower of French letters went all over the front steps. Later on, I asked my father about Sir Miles, ever so innocent like, and the reason for his lack of amusement became clear. He's evidently a magistrate and anti most things, including abortion, sex before marriage and pervy magazines and for once, I felt quite sorry for Leggett. She went down on her hands and knees, grovelling around and trying to pick them all up. She couldn't prove it, of course, but she and Fiona had had words on more than one occasion and I reckon she knew who was responsible.'

'Why are you so sure that it was Fiona? Did she tell you?'

'No, but it's just the sort of practical joke she would have gone in for and I saw Leggett staring at her after the old boy had left and if looks could kill.'

'And it was soon after that Fiona was drowned?'

'That's right.'

'You said that she was keen on riding, too.'

'You bet. She was really good, not like me. I love it, but I'm hopeless.'

'Any talent at the stables?'

'Talent? Oh, Jane, you have got it badly, haven't you? No, there isn't. There's only Mr Hockaday, and his wife won't let him out of her sight, and Joe, who's a bit simple.' Angela suddenly looked down at her watch. 'Good grief, five-thirty already. I'll just finish off the paté and then we'll have to go.'

# 6

Snowball, the white mare, was Joe Harvey's favourite and when things were getting him down, he could always relax and try to forget. When the Hockadays' daughter had started to enter for the local gymkhanas, she had won several prizes for the best turned-out horse and no wonder, he thought, as he brushed the mare's already gleaming quarters with steady rhythmical strokes.

If it hadn't been for his widowed mother, all alone apart from him and crippled by arthritis, he would have left long since, he told himself. Having to put up with that woman every day was bad enough and then, on top of that, had come the event which he was unable to get out of his mind, the night when . . .

The sun, which had been shining through the open door and had been warming his back, was suddenly obscured and he turned his head and looked over his shoulder. With the brilliant light behind her, he could only make out the silhouette of the girl in the black riding hat, shirt, breeches and boots; he stared at her open-mouthed for a moment and then let out a cry of horror as she took a step towards him.

'Joe? Joe Harvey?'

Now that she was away from the light and he had heard her speak, he realised that he had never seen her before and he sank down on to the stool, covering his face with his hands.

'I'm sorry, I thought . . . I thought . . . '

'That I was Fiona?'

He looked up at her aghast. 'Who are you? How did you know?'

'You've no need to worry about that.' The young woman came and sat down on the straw beside him. 'Why not tell me about it?'

★ ★ ★

When Joe Harvey was still at school, he used to help the Hockadays at weekends and then when he reached the age of sixteen and his father, who had worked on the farm until it had started to lose money and was abandoned, died, he welcomed the opportunity to go to them full-time. An additional inducement was the tied cottage that went with the job and which solved the problem of his mother; the stables were only ten minutes bike ride away and there was no problem about getting back and giving her lunch. He wasn't to know, though, that the cottage, which had seemed to be the answer to all their difficulties, was going to prove to be the chain that would prevent him from escaping.

Joe had always been slow with words, the others at school constantly making fun of him, and although he was now eighteen and nearly six feet tall, he had never had the chance to grow up emotionally. With his mother to look after, he had no friends of his own age and sex, let alone of the opposite one. The women, and it was nearly always the women from Croxley Hall and not the men, who used the stables, either ignored him completely, or at best ordered him about and left him a tip if he was lucky and as for the people from outside the health farm, they were practically all pre-teen girls.

Then he met Fiona. If he had been less naive, he would have realised what she was up to right at the outset; the top two buttons of her shirt which always happened to be undone, the time when her foot slipped when he was giving her a leg up on to Snowball and the fact that some soft part of her body always seemed to come into contact with him when she brought the mare back into the stable, should have made it obvious.

She had been up to her tricks again on that hot, late May afternoon and half an hour after everyone had left, he was grooming Snowball and trying to forget all about her, when he heard a whistling sound. He only just had time to begin to turn his head, when something seared the seat of his jeans and he jerked upright, letting out a cry of pure agony. Through the mist of tears that clouded his vision, he saw Fiona standing there, legs apart, her face flushed and tapping her left hand with her riding crop.

'Well, aren't you going to do anything about it? If you were half a man, you'd . . . ' The girl slowly shook her head and moistened her lips with the tip of her tongue. 'At one o'clock tomorrow morning, I'm going to ride Snowball bare . . . back in the moonlight. I expect you to have her ready.'

Joe felt the blood pounding in his temples and started towards her.

'Fiona!'

The girl looked over her shoulder. 'OK Amanda, I'm coming.' She paused at the door, took off her riding cap and shook her hair free, giving the whip a menacing swish through the air. 'You'd better be there; I might even let you get your own back.'

Joe Harvey stood there for a long time after she had gone, running his fingers over the ridge on his skin that he could feel even through the material of his jeans.

'Bitch!' he hissed through his teeth.

The idea of reporting her to the Hockadays went through his mind, but he knew that he never would and that he would be at the stables that night. It had been a hot, cloudless day and it was a cool, clear night without a whisper of wind. The nearly full moon made it brilliantly light and Joe approached the stables from the side away from the Hockadays, blessing the fact that they didn't own a dog. He was there at twelve forty-five, looked round and seeing no sign of the girl, went into Snowball's stall and gently began to pat the mare's neck. He didn't really believe that Fiona was going to come and as the minutes went by, felt the anger building up inside him. What harm had he ever done her that she should have wanted to play silly tricks on him?

'Well, get her ready — I haven't got all night.'

Joe Harvey whirled round and saw the girl framed in the doorway. She was wearing a dark track-suit and tennis shoes and snapped her fingers at him as he stood staring at her.

'Just put on the bridle and lead her out — I'll show you where to go.'

The mare's hooves on the concrete path seemed to him to be making the most appalling noise, but he soon got the horse on to the grass and followed the girl across the paddock, through the gate and into the field beyond.

'Right. Give me a leg up and stand right there.'

She slowly walked the mare round him in a wide circle, then repeated the manoeuvre at a trot and finally at a canter. Even at that moment, he had to admire how well she rode and he was just wondering if that was all it was going to be, when she cut across the circle towards him, jumped off, removed her tennis shoes and gave him a long kiss.

'Well, aren't you going to help me back on?'

Joe had never been kissed like that before and when he was still trying to get his breathing steady, she came round again. The young stable lad felt as if he was in a dream as her socks, tracksuit and finally her pants joined her shoes on the ground and he watched the pale figure on the white horse trotting round him, unable to take his eyes off her. Joe had seen pictures of naked girls — Mike Hockaday had some copies of *Penthouse* in his office — but they hadn't prepared him for the softness of her, her fragrance, the feel of her skin as he had helped her on to Snowball's back for the last time, nor the way her small, firm breasts moved up and down as the mare trotted towards him.

'Now it's your turn.'

'My turn?'

'Yes, ride a cock-horse.'

He made a half-hearted attempt to stop her, but her hands were already at the buckle of his belt and he was powerless to resist.

'My goodness, you are a big fellow.'

When the mare began to walk forwards with the two of them sitting on her back and the girl facing him, he didn't last for more than a few seconds.

'I'm sorry,' he said, 'I . . . '

'Don't worry,' she whispered in his ear, gripping him more tightly with her arms and moving her legs up behind his back, 'the second time's always better.'

She was facing him only inches away and after several minutes, and as Snowball began to trot, he saw her purse her lips and screw up her eyes. For a moment, he thought he was hurting her and made a move to stop the horse, but then he heard her harsh whisper and understood.

\* \* \*

Joe Harvey took his hands away from his eyes and Jane saw the tears streaming down his cheeks.

'If only I hadn't come here that night, it would never have happened; it was all my fault.'

'Don't be so daft and for goodness' sake stop feeling sorry for yourself. Fiona made all the running and she knew perfectly well what she was doing. If you hadn't turned up, she would as like as not gone for a swim anyway. Have you told anyone else about this?'

'No.'

'Well, now you've got it off your chest, you must forget all about it. What happened when it was all over?'

'Nothing much. She dressed, climbed over the boundary fence and ran off towards the school buildings.'

Joe Harvey hardly heard the question. He was remembering the feel of the girl as she had held him for a moment before leaving and her wave as she turned towards him before disappearing behind the tall trees that shielded the main buildings from view.

The young man looked so doleful that Jane put her arms round him and gave him a hug.

'Cheer up, Joe. It's all over now.'

She suddenly felt him stiffen, heard the step outside and hurriedly picked up the brush that Joe had dropped on to the straw.

'And what exactly do you think you're doing, Joe?'

'Nothing, Mrs Hockaday.'

'If you must know,' Jane said, 'he was showing me how to groom Snowball.'

'Huh! And that's why you've got straw all over your back, I suppose. Joe, my husband wants to see you in his office.'

The woman waited until the stable lad had gone, then advanced towards Jane, standing only three feet away. 'And now, Miss . . . ? What have you to say for yourself?'

'If you think you can bully me like you obviously enjoy bullying a young lad who can't answer back, you've got another think coming. I'm paying a great deal of money for the facilities of this place and I doubt if Mr Glover would be pleased to hear about your attitude. If I get word that anything has happened to Joe, I'll . . . '

'Are you trying to threaten me?'

'Not trying, Mrs Hockaday.'

The woman stared at Jane for a moment, then her eyes dropped, she turned on her heel and stalked out of the stall. Jane made her way back to the house deep in thought; it was the first time she had been able to act out the part of a rich, spoiled and privileged young woman, which she had decided on the spur of the moment would be the best way to deal with Mrs Hockaday and, to her shame, she had thoroughly enjoyed both the experience and her unexpectedly easy victory.

★ ★ ★

Roger Newton winced as he reached across to switch off the cassette recorder in the practically new Porsche 924 that he had persuaded Morrie Epstein to lend him. Morrie ran a rather dodgy second-hand car business and owed him a favour or two and while the detective knew very well that Kershaw wouldn't have approved of the arrangement, he could hardly, he reasoned, have turned up either in a police car, or in his own six-year-old Ford Escort. Newton was delighted with the car and would have been more so had it not been for the fact that he was getting so much pain from his shoulder; in the preceding week or two, it had got steadily worse, such that now it woke him up every time he turned over in bed.

It was curious, the detective thought, how clothes and trappings made the man. He didn't normally drive expensive sports cars or wear elegant silk squares inside hand-made shirts to set off a blazer and immaculate slacks, and yet the glance that the boy who took his suitcase gave him said it all. He had been labelled as a man of means, who wouldn't demean himself by doing anything as sordid as working, and was treated with a deference that made him squirm. The boy was bad enough, but the housekeeper, who showed him to his room, was even worse.

'We've had a number of gentlemen here, sir, who prefer to remain incognito and you can rest assured of my and indeed of all our staff's absolute discretion.'

'I rather took that for granted, Miss Leggett.' He fixed the woman with a steely stare through the monocle, which his wife Alison had insisted that he took with him, and held up his hand as she flushed and began to stammer her apologies. 'I sincerely hope that that unfortunate incident here a few weeks ago was an isolated one — publicity of that kind is something that I dislike intensely.'

'You're referring to the drowning of

one of our physiotherapists?'

'What else?'

'She was a most unstable young woman.'

'I'm sorry to hear that you put unstable young women on your staff, Miss Leggett.'

'Not my staff, sir. I have nothing to do with the physiotherapy department.'

Newton nodded. 'Well, instructive though I have found our little chat, Miss Leggett, you must excuse me — I wish to unpack.'

'Of course, sir.'

The four-course lunch of avocado pear with vinaigrette sauce, sole, lamb cutlets and a raspberry sorbet would have done justice to a top-class restaurant and Newton couldn't help chuckling to himself at the thought of what was likely to be on offer in the other dining-room. If he had been impressed by the meal, he was even more so by the standard of the medical examination that was conducted by Dr Beauchamp in the early afternoon.

'This is a most important part of the assessment,' he said, when he had asked the detective to undress after taking a detailed medical history. 'It doesn't do to recommend a particular diet or programme of physical exercise without making sure that the person is up to it, particularly as we have the sort of clientele that expects miracles.'

The physician was writing up his notes when Newton came out of the cubicle and he looked up, making a gesture towards the chair.

'It's a pleasure to find someone in relatively good shape for a change.'

'Relatively?'

The man smiled. 'It is true that you smoke, but fortunately only a pipe, you're the right weight for your height and you have a blameless family history, but there is a certain laxity in your abdominal muscles and you do have this quite nasty capsulitis around your left shoulder joint.'

'Can that be fixed? I was hoping to play some golf and at the moment I can't begin to swing a club properly.'

'You must have damaged the tendon with the over-enthusiastic use of the paint brush on that ceiling of yours and then, with the lack of use, the joint has developed what we call adhesive capsulitis, which is also sometimes known as a frozen shoulder. You have a choice; you can either let it recover of its own accord, but that could take up to a year, or we could try to mobilise it for you. Our head physiotherapist, Barbara Galton, is an expert at it, but I should warn you that the treatment is rather painful.'

The detective grinned. 'In my admittedly somewhat limited experience, if a doctor says that, it will be like all the tortures in a Hieronymus Bosch picture rolled into one, but I don't reckon that I have a great deal of choice.'

'Very well. I'll give you a note for her — no time like the present.'

The gymnasium was a hive of activity when Newton arrived; a short fat man, the top of whose bald head was glistening with sweat, was pedalling away on a static bicycle as if his life depended on it, an elderly woman, with her feet under the bottom rung of the wall bars was doing some sit-ups and a group of about a dozen was doing some exercises to music. He allowed himself the suspicion of a smile as he saw Jane Warwick at the back. Was it his imagination, or had she already shed a pound or two? She certainly looked surprisingly trim in her green tracksuit. She gave him a wink as he went by and then he was knocking on the door marked 'Superintendent Physiotherapist'.

The slim, middle-aged woman of medium height, her grey hair in a tight perm and her face devoid of make-up, shook his hand and studied the note he had brought with him.

'Well, let's see if we can find a vacant cubicle, shall we, and then I'll be able to take a look at it.'

The woman examined his shoulder with even more care than the doctor and then asked him to stand in front of the double mirror.

'Now, look. If you compare the two sides, you can see that almost all the movement you are achieving is by tricks, the joint itself is almost fixed. What we need to do is try to overcome the muscle spasm and then mobilise it. Lie down there, will you? All right, then, now relax as much as possible.'

The physiotherapist began a gentle sideways flapping motion of his arm, very gradually increasing the range of movement; it was quite soothing, pleasant even, and did nothing to prepare him for what happened a few minutes later. Miss Galton took his arm in a vice-like grip, flexed it to a right angle at the elbow and began to rotate it sideways, seemingly with all her very considerable strength. Newton could feel the sweat breaking out on his forehead and gritted his teeth to prevent himself from crying out as the appalling pain knifed through his shoulder.

'You're doing fine, just try to relax — only another minute.'

Another minute! It felt like half an hour and there was nothing he could do to suppress a groan as all the muscles around his shoulder suddenly went into spasm. The relief as she started the flapping motion again was indescribable, the pain gradually subsided and he opened his eyes.

'I'm afraid that may have stirred things up a bit; I'll give you some paracetamol to take. How does it feel now?'

'Not too bad, thanks. Much better than it did a short time ago.'

'I think perhaps we might try some ultra-sound as well. Don't worry, you won't feel anything.'

'Did I look that scared?'

Newton wasn't going to rush things, but by the afternoon of his second day, while she was giving him the relaxing exercises, he decided to move on from pleasantries about the exceptional weather and the latest news on the sporting scene.

'Do you live near here?' he asked.

'I'm resident, in fact, like most of the other staff except for the doctor.'

'It must be a bit isolated.'

'I love it.' He was surprised by the intensity with which she said it. 'I like the work, as well as the surroundings and I'm planning to write a history of the chapel; it's very interesting, you know, a lot older than the present house, which was largely rebuilt after a fire in the late eighteenth century.'

'I must take a look at it. Does it have an organ? They're one of my hobbies.'

'Yes, but I'm afraid I don't know whether or not it's anything special. Mr Milroy's the person to ask about that — he plays it regularly.'

'Mr Milroy?'

'He's the estate manager and lives with his wife in a cottage in the grounds.' The woman straightened up. 'Well, that's about it for today. Does it feel any better?'

'Yes, thanks, quite a bit. Would it do any harm to swing a golf club gently?'

'Not provided you don't overdo it, but I'd better see what it involves. Why not show me with this?'

She handed him one of the ash walking sticks from the nearby rack and watched as he took a few tentative swings, gradually increasing the arc.

'It's a great deal better than when I last tried.'

'I think it would be quite good exercise for you, but you will keep to your pain-free range, won't you? I won't be here tomorrow — Celia will be able to give you the ultra-sound and then I'll continue with the mobilisation on Saturday morning.'

Roger Newton profoundly hoped that Jane Warwick had made more progress than him. He had been intending to get Barbara Galton talking a bit more, perhaps by asking her out for a drink one evening, but now the wretched woman was going off for the day and that meant that there was going to be precious little time before the meeting he had arranged on the Sunday evening with Jane and George Wainwright. He glanced at his watch; there were a couple of free hours before dinner and that, he thought, would be just nice time in which to hit a few balls on the practice ground which had been fashioned out of one of the fields abutting the riding school.

Even though it was on a modest scale, the maximum length was only about a hundred and fifty yards, like everything else at Croxley Hall, it was in immaculate condition. The distances from the hole were marked out and rubber mats placed on the turf at intervals, while the tee at the back was enclosed on three sides by a thick hedge. Newton walked up to the green, which had also been carefully tended, and after practising his putting for a few minutes, tried a number of bunker shots and then retreated to the hundred and twenty yard mark and selected his nine iron. It went better than he had been expecting and after a few easy swings, he couldn't resist putting the ball down on the turf to one side of the mat. This time, he punched down hard, took the ball first, then a divot and felt the enormous satisfaction of the perfectly timed shot. The ball sailed over the flag, landed six feet beyond it, took one bounce forward and then spun back to within eighteen inches of the hole.

'Great shot.'

The detective turned towards the man who was standing a few yards away and gave him a smile.

'Thanks.'

'I wish I could get backspin like that — I've been trying without success for years.' He walked up to the detective, extending his hand. 'Milroy, Derek Milroy. I'm the estate manager here.'

'Roger Newton.'

'I mustn't interrupt your practice.'

'Don't worry, it's not as if I was going at it very seriously — just trying out my shoulder. I have been undergoing something of an ordeal at the hands of your Miss Galton; all in a good cause, of course, and she has made remarkable progress with it, but it has been hellish painful.'

'Yes, I've heard that she is very good and I'll be sorry to see her go.'

'Go?'

'Yes, Mr Glover is starting another and bigger clinic in Northamptonshire and is anxious for her to get the physiotherapy department into shape.' He shook his head. 'I ought not to have let that piece of information slip — she doesn't know herself yet. Mr Glover's going to tell her tomorrow.'

'Don't worry, I won't say a word to anyone.'

Milroy smiled his thanks. 'I say, I hope you won't think it the most frightful cheek as we've only just met, but you wouldn't like a round with me on Sunday morning, would you? I belong to a place about ten miles from here and there's quite a decent little course; you might also like to take a bite of lunch with me and my wife afterwards. Nothing elaborate — just the three of us.'

'I'd like nothing better, but I doubt if I'll be able to hit much more than a five iron.'

'By the look of you, that's just about the sort of handicap I'm going to need. Are you game for an early start?'

'You name the time and I'll be there.'

'Shall we say eight o'clock at my cottage?'

Newton watched the man out of sight; of medium build, with dark, wavy hair and wearing a blazer, regimental tie, cavalry twill trousers and his brown shoes polished to a brilliant shine, he had ex-army officer written all over him. The detective knew the type well and had no intention of getting involved in a game with large side stakes — there was far too good a chance of being hustled. The family finances were not exactly precarious, but there wasn't all that much to spare.

Although Newton was only too well aware of the need to press on with the enquiry, there was nothing he could do about Miss Galton's absence, and the Friday passed agreeably enough with a workout in the gym, a lengthy session on the practice ground, sharpening up his short iron play and a couple of games of chess with a very fat politician. The man was desperately trying to take his mind off all the delectable things that he had heard were on offer in the non-slimmers' dining-room, but it was a losing battle, his concentration wasn't up to it and the detective won both of them comfortably.

It was immediately obvious that something had happened to upset Barbara Galton very seriously indeed; the woman almost seemed to have shrunk and looked pale and preoccupied. In contrast to the care with which she had treated him before, her efforts on that Saturday morning were perfunctory and she didn't even take the trouble to position his arm correctly. Was this the time to get her talking? One glance at her face and the fact that there were other patients in the adjoining cubicles ruled that out but, later on, when having had a swim and on his way back to the house, he saw her walking slowly across the lawn, he decided that the opportunity was too good to miss. He altered course and was walking along a narrow path flanked by rhododendrons, when he heard voices just ahead.

'Hello, Barbara, why not come and join me?'

The detective stopped dead, then crept up behind a beech tree and looked round it. Only a few yards from him there was a clearing and he saw Pat Pennington sitting on a garden seat. The superintendent physiotherapist hesitated and then she walked across to the other woman.

'All right, but I'm afraid I'll be very poor company.'

'Why? Whatever's the matter?'

Miss Galton rested her hand lightly on her labrador's head and it began to thump the ground gently with its tail.

'It's being done tactfully enough and another job has been found for me, but that can't disguise the fact that I'm being kicked out.'

'Kicked out?'

'Mr Glover started out by saying that he wanted someone of my experience to start up the physiotherapy unit in the new residential clinic he's opening in Northamptonshire, but when I explained that I was quite happy here and didn't want to move, the real reason became apparent. As he put it, I've become accident prone; he was prepared to accept that the Ruth Lavington episode was bad luck, but Fiona Graham and then the anonymous letter was the last straw as far as he was concerned.'

'Anonymous letter?'

'Yes. He didn't go so far as to show it to me, but however delicately he chose to put it, the message was quite clear. It's so unfair. Just because Fiona chose to go for a midnight swim in the nude and I happened to find her ... It's so easy to make an accusation like that and mud clings.'

'I know. Poor Barbara. It's rotten, really rotten for you. I feel so sorry for whoever sent it — they must be very disturbed.'

'I'm not in the least sorry for them and

it doesn't require a genius to guess who was responsible; Dorothy has never liked me and . . . '

'Don't say that, Barbara. You don't know that she was the one who sent it.'

'I wish I had your ability to see good in everyone.'

'Are you going to accept Mr Glover's offer?'

'What alternative have I got? An industrial tribunal with all the attendant publicity? That would hardly be a practical proposition even if I could have faced it — it's not as if I'm being dismissed. I'm too old to start yet again and I don't think I can face another new department.'

'You'll be all right, Barbara dear, look what you've achieved here. Don't worry, have a good cry — it'll do you good.'

Newton crept away, embarrassed, as the superintendent physiotherapist broke down and the other woman took her in her arms to comfort her.

# 7

It had all the promise of being yet another scorching day and Roger Newton assembled his trolley, removed all the wooden clubs from the bag before strapping it on and then took a few practice swings with his three iron, grimacing with pain as he followed through. It didn't augur very well for the game, but he couldn't back out at this late stage and it would give him a chance to get the feel of Milroy as a person. He walked round to the cottage to find the estate manager waiting for him by the side of a battered Hillman Hunter estate car.

''Morning,' the man said, giving him a cheerful grin. 'How's the arm?'

'So, so. Stiffened up a bit in the night.'

'In that case, you won't want to be humping your clubs about. Allow me.'

Milroy put the equipment into the back then slammed the tail-gate shut with a force that made the whole car shake.

'Sorry about that — Delilah isn't in the first flush of youth. In fact, I reckon that she's within three months of her final demise; that's when her next MOT test is due and my pet garage man, who's rather a soft touch in that department, has just gone out of business. I'd like to be able to say that I could afford something a little less sedate, but it looks like another old banger, if that.'

The starter motor turned the engine over with painful slowness and then quite suddenly it burst into life with a roar that would have done credit to a Chieftain tank.

'Hold tight.'

There was an ominous clunk from the automatic gear-box as he pushed the lever into drive and the old car lurched forward and shot down the drive, the transmission whining hideously.

'It's always interesting until it comes off the choke.'

Newton was more than glad that the journey lasted no more than twenty-five minutes; a smell like burning gum-boots was coming from somewhere under his feet, the vehicle lurched and wallowed whenever they turned a corner and Milroy drove with scant regard to the state of the road ahead, talking animatedly the whole time and frequently gesturing with one hand and looking towards the detective whenever he made a point.

Newton was rather hoping that Milroy's golf would turn out to be as erratic as his driving and even though the man's tee shot at the first hole went a full two hundred and fifty yards, bisecting the fairway, the detective doubted very much if he would be able to keep it up. He had noticed a distinct looseness of the grip at the top of the man's back swing, which looked as if it might prove vulnerable under pressure.

Normally, the drive was the strongest part of Newton's game and it was extremely frustrating to have to hit three quarter four iron shots off the tee and he usually finished a good eighty yards adrift. On most of the par four holes he was unable to get up in two, but he was determined not to let the man beat him without a struggle and concentrated all he knew on his short game. He lost the first hole to a four, but after they had halved the short second, Milroy came off one of his slashing drives and the high slice disappeared into thick rough. Even though he recovered well to put the ball back on to the fairway, the detective got down in two from just off the green and won the hole in a four to a five.

Newton's downfall came at the eighteenth when they were all square. The hole was a dog-leg to the left and after Milroy had hit another immensely long and straight drive, the detective risked a full three iron off the tee in an attempt to make the angle of the dog-leg. A tearing pain went through his shoulder at the very top of his back swing and although he tried to go through with the shot, his timing was awry and the ball travelled no more than a hundred and forty yards, failing to reach the fairway. He did manage to make a reasonable recovery, but was short in three and despite another good pitch and putt, lost the hole and the match to a steady four from his opponent.

'Well played,' he said as they shook hands. 'Straight and long when it really mattered.'

Milroy was like a dog with two tails and was still talking about it on their way back to his cottage.

'They're tricky those graphite shafts, but, by God, when you really catch one, it certainly goes.'

'I wish I could have tried one out.'

'You shall, my dear fellow — I'll give instructions to Miss Galton that she must get you fighting fit by the end of the week. I'll need a few strokes then — that's for certain.'

Despite the fact that they had had a drink in the clubhouse after their round, it was only a few minutes after twelve when they got back to Croxley Hall.

'Why not change and freshen up and I'll look forward to seeing you back here just before one?'

'Fine.'

'Oh, by the way, it's terribly rude of me, but I forgot to tell you that I have to catch the three-thirty for London — a meeting with our Treasurer. He's one of those ghastly people who go in for working breakfasts, so I always travel up the night before and stay at my club.' He raised his eyebrows. 'It's a penance I have to undertake the third Monday of every month. Will you forgive me if I leave at about three?'

'Of course.'

Newton had ample time in which to shower, change and make a phone call before returning to the cottage.

'Ah, there you are.' Milroy led the way into the hall and made a gesture towards the door on the other side. 'Pre-lunch drink outside suit you? I was thinking of mixing a jug of Pimm's.'

'I can't imagine anything better.'

The detective stepped out on to the patio, which was paved with variegated stones, and looked at the small rectangle of lawn with rose bushes on three sides of it. The whole was enclosed by a wall and blended perfectly with the Cotswold stone cottage, the tall trees in the distance and the tower of the chapel a hundred yards away to their right.

'What a lovely spot! It's quite perfect.'

'We think so, too. Why not take a seat while I fix the drinks?'

Newton moved the garden chair into the one patch of shade and looked up at the cloudless sky. Magnificent weather, regular exercise in the gym, a little gentle golf and haute cuisine, there was little doubt that the place was hardly conductive to work and he only hoped that Jane had managed to make more progress than he had. He was idly watching a vapour trail in the sky when Milroy came back carrying a tray, on which was resting a superb cut-glass jug containing a delicious looking liquid, in which were floating slices of apple, orange and lemon, and two equally ornate glasses.

'Not to strong, I hope.'

Newton stirred the ice cold drink and took a sip. 'No, just right.'

'Apologies for taking so long; the fact is that Louise has been stricken by one of her migraines. She so wanted to meet you, but I'm afraid that bed in a darkened room is the only answer.'

'I am sorry.'

'Wretched thing, isn't it? You'd have

thought that the medical profession would have come up with the answer by now, wouldn't you? The poor girl has tried everything including all that currently fashionable fringe stuff — special foods to avoid allergy are her latest fad. Personally, I think it's a complete waste of time and money, but she seems to have faith in it and one can hardly blame her when she's laid low every couple of weeks or so. Excuse me for a moment — don't want to overcook the spuds.'

The lunch was delicious. Salmon, salad and new potatoes were followed by strawberries and cream and during it, Milroy kept up a stream of anecdotes about his army service and some of his bizarre experiences in Germany after the war.

'You must find life here a bit tame after all that.'

'Oh, I don't know. We have our little domestic excitements from time to time and one can't retain the fires of youth for ever.' He waved his hand towards the garden. 'There are other compensations as well, as you can see.' He suddenly turned and looked very directly at the detective. 'And what do you do for a living, old man?'

Newton had been anticipating that question and had been wondering when Milroy would get round to it.

'You could say that I was a student of human nature.'

He was saved from further explanation by the loud thump that came from the room directly above and the fact that Milroy immediately jumped to his feet and went quickly up the stairs.

'Nothing seriously amiss, I'm happy to report,' he said when he got back. 'Just the bedside lamp falling off the table when Louise reached for her tablets.'

If Newton managed to parry the man's attempts at probing into what he did for a living, Milroy was equally adept at avoiding Croxley Hall gossip and they soon settled for talk about golf and the various courses on which they had played.

'Good Lord! Ten to three already,' Milroy said, when he had finished chuckling at one of Newton's stories about the President's Putter. 'Do forgive me, I must be off.'

'Of course. Thank you for a memorable game and a delicious lunch. We must have a return later in the week and if you know of a suitable place, I'd like to return your hospitality.'

'You're too kind. The gate at the bottom of the garden is the quickest route.'

The detective glanced over his shoulder as he walked in the direction of the main buildings and for a fleeting second he saw someone watching him from one of the upstairs windows before the face was suddenly withdrawn and the curtain fell back into place. It was pleasantly cool in the wood and Newton sat down on the stump of a beech tree and reached for his tobacco pouch, only to let out a muffled curse as he realised where he had left it. He could hardly go back just when Milroy was on the point of leaving. At almost the same moment that he heard the roar of the Hillman's exhaust, he had another, and much better, idea and stepped behind the trunk of a massive oak tree until the car had passed by.

The detective sat there deep in thought for another ten minutes and then made his way back to the cottage, walking slowly up the path and ringing the bell. After what seemed an interminable delay, Louise Milroy came to the door; she was wearing a crumpled dressing-gown and it was only too obvious what she had been doing and that his guess had been correct. Her hair was all over the place, her speech was slurred and she began to giggle when she saw the detective's expression.

'I'm sorry to disturb you, but I foolishly left my tobacco pouch behind.'

'There's no need to apologise, no one else does.'

Through the open kitchen door, Newton could see the pile of dirty crockery on the draining board and quickly averted his gaze when the woman let out a harsh laugh.

'You didn't really imagine that I was going to wash up for the pair of you, did you?'

'Why don't you go into the sitting-room

while I deal with it and then I'll get you a cup of tea.'

'Now I get it; you fancy me, is that it? Go ahead if that's what you want. Derek won't mind, he's had most of the younger female members of staff here.'

Before the detective could move, she threw open her dressing-gown and let out another mirthless laugh.

'Revolting sight, isn't it? Withered breasts and sagging stomach and how about this attractive feature?'

She traced the uneven purple scar that ran downwards from her umbilicus with her forefinger and then began to cry almost silently, the tears coursing down her cheeks, leaving twin dark tracks as her mascara ran. Newton wrapped the dressing-gown around her, led her into the living-room, helped her on to the sofa and went out again quickly. When he looked in once more some ten minutes later, the woman was snoring gently, her mouth hanging open, and after he had finished in the kitchen, she was still fast asleep. The opportunity was too good to miss and after hesitating for a moment at the doorway, he ran up the stairs.

Louise Milroy's room was in predictable disarray, the bed unmade, an empty bottle of gin stuffed only half out of sight and clothes strewn all over the floor; but her husband's was the exact opposite, everything being neatly in its place. He raised his eyebrows at the contents of the wardrobe and chest of drawers, examining a couple of the suits carefully. He wasn't expecting to find any papers or letters — he assumed that they would all be safely behind the locked door of the study on the ground floor — and after having a quick look at the spare bedroom, he went into the bathroom. The full, unopened bottle of gin was in the very first place he went to — the lavatory cistern. The detective let out a sigh; one of these days someone was going to think of somewhere original.

Louise Milroy didn't look as if she had stirred since his last visit and when he put down the tea-tray and shook her hard by the shoulder, she opened one blood-shot eye and struggled to sit up.

'What? You still here?'

'I thought you might like a hot drink.'

Several minutes went by before she was properly awake and then she took a cautious sip from her cup.

'You can't imagine what it's like living in this dump all the year round,' she said a long time later, all of a sudden looking more animated. 'I suppose it might just about be all right if your only interests are riding, swimming and making yourself look ridiculous in a gym, but as to anything worthwhile, any culture ... My God, have you taken a look at the staff here? Philistines the lot of them. It wasn't always like this, you know; we lived in style when Derek was in the army.'

'Why did he leave?'

'Got caught having it away with the Colonel's daughter. If it had been his wife, he wouldn't have minded — she'd been ridden by more officers than the regimental charger — but of course Derek had to select the virginal Claire and that meant having to resign. After that, he managed to dispose of most of my money on one crack-brained scheme after another until we finally finished up here.'

'But you don't seem to be doing all that badly; this is a very nice house and your husband's got a good job.'

'You call this a nice house? You, who must have pots of money? If I tell you that my father's an earl, perhaps you can understand what I mean. That's just about the only reason why Derek didn't push off long ago — he wouldn't want to upset the prospect of lots of lovely lolly coming our way when the old man dies, would he? You'd better watch out yourself; Derek's a crashing snob, which is why he's trying to cultivate you. The poor fool thinks that you're a peer in disguise and he's just longing to have a go in that Porsche of yours. Typical of Derek to be taken in by the top dressing, he always was gullible. You're no peer, no man of any breeding would have been so insufferably bourgeois as to have done the washing up. You're every bit as phoney as Derek — I can spot that sort of thing a mile off — but it looks as if you're better than him at falling on your feet.

'All things considered, though, I suppose you could say that he didn't do badly; the reason why he got this job in the first place was because some years ago he happened to find Glover's current fancy boyfriend unconscious by the side of a ski run. I'll say this for Derek, he could ski, and it was child's play for him to get the boy down, but of course he made the most of it, playing the hero and struggling down with him after dark. If you ask me, he might even have set it up, knocking the youth out just so that he could soften Glover up as an insurance policy for the future. Sure enough, when the balloon did go up, Glover was good for this job and the cottage, not to mention those fancy clothes you no doubt saw when you went upstairs.' The woman laughed. 'I'm not quite so far gone as you no doubt thought.' She had another of her abrupt changes of mood and the tears started to appear again. 'I even had a job here myself; I was the secretary until that frightful dyke of a woman, Galton, had me dismissed for drinking and that nauseating goody-goody Pat Pennington took over. Since then, I've had no part in it and have had to put up with rags to wear, not to mention sitting here while Derek goes on 'business trips' to London.'

'Why don't you accompany him?'

'He wouldn't have that; it would stop him having a good time with those fancy women of his. Anyway, Glover has a thing about alcohol — he's a teetotaller himself — which is why he kicked me out of my job here and he wouldn't countenance any risk of me blotting my copybook with any of his business cronies. You're wondering why I haven't walked out?'

'It did cross my mind.'

'I bet it did. You're on the fiddle yourself, aren't you? Does Derek owe you money? Is that why you were on the prowl upstairs? Never mind, where was I? Oh, yes. Why didn't I leave long ago? The answer's quite simple, I've got nowhere else to go; my father set up a trust fund and I get a bit of income provided I don't make a fuss and keep out of the family's way. Charming, isn't it?' Louise Milroy got unsteadily to her feet and reached behind the screen in front of the fireplace, pulling out a half empty bottle of gin and putting the opening to her mouth. 'At least the money's enough to keep me supplied with the necessary.' She raised the bottle in mock salute. 'Don't worry, Derek knows all about it — it's just a silly little game we play, like me pretending not to know what he does when he goes up to London. I knew he'd find someone else after that girl got nicked for having snow in her room. Typical of Derek to have had the luck not to get caught with her. They also used to smoke pot together — I've still got a sense of smell and I could always tell when he'd been with her.'

'Was Ruth Lavington a particular friend of his, then?'

The woman looked up sharply at the detective. 'How did you know her name?'

'Gossip in the physiotherapy department.'

'Didn't they tell you, then, that Derek was always nipping out at night to meet her; he thought I didn't know about that, but I don't sleep as much as people think.'

The woman lifted the bottle once more, took another stiff drink and lay down on the sofa.

'Why are you so sure that he's found a replacement?'

'Of course he has; Derek never could give it a rest and he's still leaving me alone, isn't he? Now I'm shocking you.' The woman giggled. 'Where do you think you're going?'

Newton paused at the door, the tray in his hands. 'Just off to sharpen my bourgeois skills.'

★ ★ ★

'What's wrong with you?'

Jane Warwick wrinkled her nose. 'I'm sorry, it's the smell and sight of those sausages — I'm starving.'

Newton grinned as he saw the anguished expression on the young woman's face. 'You mustn't weaken just when you're in sight of victory — you're looking positively sylphlike already.'

'That reminds me,' Wainwright said. 'I missed my supper in order to get back here in time.' The sergeant made his way to the bar and came back with the menu. 'Steak and kidney pie and mashed potato will just about do to start with — sure you won't change your mind?'

'I'd just love a . . . '

'Temptations were made to be resisted. Jane here is on a very strict diet, George, a very strict one indeed and you mustn't sabotage her noble efforts. I think she might just be allowed a slimline tonic, if you'd be so kind, and George?'

'Yes, sir.'

'It might be more tactful if you fed the inner man out of sight and sound and just as importantly, out of smell as well. And get a move on, will you? It's only an hour short of closing time.'

When the massive man departed to the far corner of the saloon, Newton reckoned that he would have had a mutiny on his hands if Jane hadn't had her back to him. As they discussed what each of them had discovered, over his shoulder, he could see Wainwright demolishing an enormous plateful of delicious looking food and by its side, apple pie and custard waiting to follow suit.

'Ah, George, finished at last? Come and sit down and I'll try to give you a summary of where we've got to so far.' He flicked back the pages of his notebook. 'We have a young and distinctly libidinous physiotherapist, who likes her greens, and who is not averse to playing rather malicious practical jokes. She is scared of water and is found dead in the swimming pool after having had sex on the back of a white horse with one slightly dim stable lad.' Newton looked up. 'What's the matter, George? Don't tell me that at long last you've got indigestion. No? Good. Well, in the immortal words of Magnus Magnusson: 'I've started, so I'll finish'. An occupational therapist from the same department has a penchant both for drugs of various sorts and gorillas and despite being put inside for the former, seems to have fallen on her feet. Miss Galton, accused at best of being unlucky and at worst of having an unhealthy interest in her female staff, is being elbowed out with the help of our friend, the anonymous letter writer, and there seem to be tensions between her, the domestic supervisor and Milroy's wife, who was at one time the secretary here and is now a drunken wreck. I make it sound like 'Cold Comfort Farm', don't I?' The detective could see that he was losing his audience and decided to continue, leaving out the literary allusions. 'Now, Milroy I find interesting. He drives a terrible old car and yet has Savile Row suits in his wardrobe and a set of very expensive graphite shafted golf clubs. Have I left anything out, Jane?'

'I don't think so, but the way you put it doesn't give at all a fair impression of the place. It's extremely well run and obviously successful.'

'Yes, you're quite right, I'm afraid I was being flippant, as usual. George, how did you get on with Milroy?'

'Nothing much to report. He drove to Cheltenham in that old rattle-trap, left it in the station car park and then took the train to Paddington.'

'And where did he go then? No, don't tell us. Jane?'

Newton made an elaborate show of

conducting an orchestra as they said 'St John's Wood' together, then laughed as he saw his assistant's bewildered expression.

'Don't worry, George, we haven't got second sight — a gorilla told us.'

'A gorilla?' Wainwright turned towards Jane. 'And what are you giggling about?'

'I'm afraid that you were too gently nurtured to be able to understand the joke, George,' Newton said.

'I don't know what you're both on about; he didn't go anywhere near St John's Wood, he took a cab straight to a club in Piccadilly.'

'Oh, he did, did he? My apologies, George, serves me right for trying to be too clever. Jane, would you mind going over Joe's story again for George's benefit? That lad must be the number one suspect and if, by any chance, Fiona was teasing him, anything might have happened.'

Newton studied his notes while she again described what the boy had told her.

'Well, what do you make of it, George?'
'I reckon he made all that stuff up. He

probably raped her and then threw her into the pool, hoping that it would look like an accident. From what you've said about that Graham girl, I can't see her being interested in a village idiot.'

'That's not fair. Joe may not have had much education, but he's not that stupid and he's also very nice looking. Anyway, his story fits in very well with Dr Golding's report.'

'You have a good point there, Jane.' Newton tapped his teeth with his ball-point pen. 'I suppose she might have made fun of him after it was all over, he could have lost his temper, clobbered her, thought he'd killed her and then set up the scenario at the pool.'

'That doesn't ring true to me, either,' Jane said. 'I mean, I could just about see Joe losing control if he had been sexually humiliated, but not then to act in such a calculated manner.'

'Maybe you're right. And what about that Mrs Hockaday?'

'She was certainly extremely aggressive and rude to me.'

'Did you think she was interested in Joe?'

'Sexually, you mean?'
'Yes.'
'I wouldn't know about that, but he was certainly scared stiff of her.'
'This Joe certainly requires a bit more research and I'll tackle that tomorrow. George, will you see what you can dig up on Milroy? The army might be as good a place to start as any.'
'How about me?'
'You, my dear Jane, deserve a rest — you've done practically all the work so far.'

# 8

Roger Newton, having spent the Monday morning having his treatment with Miss Galton, doing some stomach muscle strengthening exercises in the gym and spending an hour on the practice ground, went into lunch well pleased with his progress. The arc of his golf swing had increased substantially and he had even been able to hit a few reasonable shots with his four wood, using a plastic ball. He was in a mellow mood and when, after lunch, Colonel Massingham, who was sitting in the shade in a deckchair, beckoned to him, he made no attempt to take evasive action.

'Bring your coffee over here, my dear fellow; it's far too hot in the sun — worse than Tobruk in forty-one.'

The detective did as he was bid, pulling up a garden seat.

'How's the cycling going, Colonel?'

'Managed ten miles this morning.' The

man leaned across and spoke in a hoarse whisper, his face flushed with excitement. 'You know that girl in my class, the one with the big . . . '

'Jane Warwick, you mean,' Newton said hurriedly.

'Yes, that's the filly. Used to be good with names at one time — losin' me grip.'

'What about her?'

'You've heard the rumour that she's something big in the pop music world?' Newton nodded — the stories that had been floating around about both of them had been a constant source of amusement to him. 'Well, I think it must be true. I mean, how else could a girl of that age, who's well enough spoken, but obviously not a member of the county set, come by the resources to be able to afford to stay here?' The man frowned. 'Now, where was I?'

'You appeared to be about to tell me something about Jane Warwick.'

'Ah, yes, so I was — told you I was slippin'. She's disappeared.'

The colonel had certainly been expecting something a bit more than a polite expression of interest at his news, but not for Newton to straighten up so abruptly that he knocked his coffee cup on to the grass.

'She's what?'

'Disappeared.'

'Are you sure?'

'She generally sits next to me in that starvation hall they have the effrontery to call a dining-room at lunch time today, there she wasn't, neither was she in the gym this morning. The waitress, who's always good for a gossip, told me that her bed hadn't been slept in and that she hadn't been seen since supper-time yesterday. What? Not off already?'

''Fraid so — urgent business.'

The detective hurried across to the front entrance and found Miss Leggett in her office.

'You are acting director here, I understand,' he said crisply before the woman had time to get out of her chair.

'That's right, sir. Nothing wrong, I hope.'

'Is it true that Miss Warwick is missing?'

'Well, missing is altogether too strong a

word; it's true that she didn't sleep here last night, but this isn't a convent, you know, and if one of our guests . . . '

'Miss Warwick wouldn't have left here without telling me,' Newton handed his warrant card across. 'I am a police officer and I was keeping an eye on her.'

'Then she is someone important?'

'I want a thorough search made of all the buildings and the grounds as well. I've no wish to embarrass you with unnecessary publicity, so I suggest that you organise it yourself.'

'I'll see to it right away. I'll get Miss Pennington to help me — she's totally trustworthy.'

'Very well. I'll be back here at five for a report. You needn't worry about the stables, I'll go there myself.' Newton saw the woman's lips twitch. 'Did you wish to say anything else, Miss Leggett?'

'Mrs Hockaday did tell me the other day that Joe and Miss Warwick were . . . '

'Were what, Miss Leggett?'

'Er, having a conversation at the stables.'

★ ★ ★

Newton decided that it would be tactful to approach the Hockadays before speaking to Joe, but regretted it within minutes of having met the two of them; to have said that they were unenthusiastic about the idea would have been a wild understatement.

'I have no wish to be in any way obstructive, Inspector, but ... ' Mrs Hockaday began and the detective let out an internal sigh of resignation, having long since given up any attempt at keeping a count of the number of times he had heard that particular form of rebuff. ' ... Joe only has a crippled mother, who, to be honest, is about as dim as he is, and I feel he needs someone to look after his interests.'

'You make it sound as if he has something to hide,' Newton said. 'Anyway, he is eighteen and should be capable of answering for himself.'

'I don't know what all the fuss is about. A young woman, no doubt with more money than sense, has decided to take off and to my mind that's no reason to hound someone like Joe.'

Newton was normally immune to remarks like that, but for once the woman's arrogance and thinly-veiled contempt caught him on the raw.

'In the first place, I don't care for the word hound, secondly, I'm quite certain that she hasn't taken off, as you put it, and finally, may I remind you that it was you who told Miss Leggett that Joe and Miss Warwick were chatting together in the stables last week. Young Joe also has something else to explain and I'd be grateful if you'd tell me where he is.'

'I don't like your attitude, Inspector, and I've a good mind to . . . '

'If there's any special reason why you think that Joe needs protecting, it might be wise to tell me. Are you really trying to maintain that not upsetting a young man is more important than the life of a young woman?'

'That's being more than a bit melodramatic, isn't it?'

'I assure you that it isn't; Joe may have some information and I'm much more likely to find out if he does know anything if I see him quietly on his own without a third party being present.'

'Look here, Inspector . . .'

'Pamela, leave this to me, will you?' Newton looked round in surprise at Hockaday, who up to that moment, had hardly said a word. 'Of course you must see him, Inspector, he's . . .'

'Michael . . .'

'He's in the stables cleaning up.'

The couple were shooting malignant glances at one another and the detective would have given a good deal to have been a fly on the wall and to have heard what they said after he had left. He wasn't expecting Hockaday to show him to the front gate, either.

'You mustn't take any notice of my wife,' the man said, 'she's really been a mother to Joe — we weren't able to have more than one child and she always wanted a son — and she does get rather possessive at times. You will go easy on him, though, won't you? He's very young for his age.'

'Don't worry, I will. Thanks for your help.'

Newton walked slowly towards the

stables feeling that he had made a complete mess of his interview with the Hockadays, but wondering, nevertheless, if the woman's attitude hadn't been a bit more than just that of a mother hen. Did she know something more about Joe that she wasn't admitting? He found the young man hosing down the yard outside the stalls and went up to him briskly, holding out his hand.

'Roger Newton,' he said. 'You must be Joe Harvey. I wanted your help over the young lady with whom you had a talk last week — she's disappeared.'

'You from the police?'

'That's right. I'm trying to see everyone who's known to have spoken to her in the day or two before it happened.'

When the young man looked over his shoulder, Newton wondered for a moment if he was going to make a run for it, but then he glanced back at the detective and all the tension suddenly went out of him.

'Are you going to arrest me?'

'Good heavens no — whatever gave you that idea? Why don't we go over there and take the weight off our feet — mine are killing me.' Newton waited until they were both sitting on the top rung of the wooden fence before continuing. 'It must have been from about here that you said goodbye to Fiona Graham the night she was drowned.'

Joe Harvey went deathly pale and looked for a moment as if he was going to faint, wiping the beads of perspiration off his forehead, but then he took a grip of himself and turned to stare defiantly at the detective.

'How did you know that?'

'Someone overheard you talking to that young woman, Jane, in the stables last week. You saw Jane again on Sunday night, didn't you?' Even before the boy nodded miserably, Newton was quite sure that his hunch had proved correct. 'Now look, Joe, you're a very important witness and I want you to tell me exactly what happened and then not repeat it to a living soul. Do you understand?'

Joe wasn't exactly articulate and it was obvious that he was still profoundly shaken by how much the detective seemed to know, but once he had been reassured that he wasn't about to be taken into immediate custody, it all came out.

\* \* \*

At the time, Joe Harvey had found it a tremendous relief at long last to be able to tell someone about that night with Fiona but, later that evening, in the privacy of his room, he began to regret it bitterly. The other young woman — he didn't even know her name — would be bound to tell her friends, it would get all over Croxley Hall and then he would lose his job.

Just as bad as that, was the fact that memories of that night, which he thought he had at last got out of his mind, came flooding back and sleep wouldn't come. The one consolation was that a gymkhana was going to be held on the riding school's land shortly, which kept him busy, and when neither Mrs Hockaday nor anyone else said anything to him, his confidence began to return. Late on the Sunday afternoon, he had just finished setting out the treble on the jumping course and was making sure that it was in line, when he heard the soft voice behind him and whirled round.

'Hello, Joe.' The young woman looked towards the jumps and gave him a smile. 'You're doing a terrific job on this — it must be terribly hard work.'

Joe Harvey flushed with a mixture of pleasure and embarrassment; he wasn't used to praise, rather the reverse, Mrs Hockaday was always finding something to criticise. He had recognised the young woman at once from her voice — he had been so upset before in the stable that he hadn't taken in her appearance properly — but he did so now. She was plumper than the other one, but no less attractive.

'I didn't have a chance to introduce myself before; my name's Jane Warwick and I'm trying to find out how Fiona died.'

'Are you a relative or something?'

'I'd like to meet you at the stables tonight at exactly the same time and in exactly same way as you did with Fiona, even to the extent of taking

Snowball out into the field. That sort of thing often jogs people's memory. You will help me, won't you Joe? I know I can rely on you.'

Joe watched her walk away, just able to make out the line of her pants under her tight slacks. In the first few days after his experience with Fiona, he had been quite unable to get it out of his mind, reliving it time and time again, and he hadn't believed that anything like that would ever happen to him again, but why else, he wondered, would this young woman want to meet him again? He didn't believe her story about wanting to find out about Fiona's death — surely, that was just an excuse. Would she feel the same, would she be softer, in less of a hurry, would she . . . ?

Joe tried everything he knew to get any thought of Jane out of his mind, working late into the evening, putting up more of the jumps, grooming the ponies and then going to bed early. It didn't work; although he told himself any number of times that he wasn't going to go, he was drawn to the field like a moth to a flame and just as the chapel clock struck one, he was once more waiting by the massive oak tree just by the paddock.

Joe had just moved his position so that he could get a better view of the main building, when he saw her. He had thought about that episode with Fiona so many times that for a moment he wasn't sure whether the girl in the tracksuit was real or not. His fantasy, reinforced by constant repetition, his half-belief in the existence of ghosts and his hopes and fears about the new girl, were all hopelessly mixed up and he watched, quite unable to move as she went into the stables and after calling out his name softly and waiting there for ten minutes, walked across the field. She stood in the middle of it for some time and then went towards the fence. She climbed over at precisely the same point that Fiona had used — he had counted the number of uprights from the gate — and then disappeared towards the chapel. The spell was broken and he sprinted after her, being on the point of calling out when the shaft of light suddenly came through the trees and he turned, without pausing, running flat out back to his bicycle and the safety of the cottage and his bedroom.

* * *

'Are you quite sure that you saw a light?' Newton asked.

'Yes, absolutely. I saw one, too, after Fiona left me; it was coming from the same place. I didn't pay any attention to it at the time, but last night reminded me of it.'

'Would you point out the direction for me, please?'

Joe jumped down off the fence and they walked some fifty yards obliquely to their right.

'It came from over there,' he said, pointing towards a gap in the trees.

'Good man — you've very observant. Now look, Joe, if anyone else, anyone at all, asks you about this, don't tell them anything and then let me know who it was. Got that straight?'

'Yes, I think so.'

Newton gave him a pat on the

shoulder. 'I knew as soon as I saw you that I could depend on you.'

The detective watched Joe Harvey out of sight and then began to stroll towards the gap in the trees. Only twenty yards ahead of the large oak was the porch of the chapel and he went straight up to the door and tried the iron handle. It was locked and after he had walked swiftly around the outside, he strode off towards the main building.

'Well, have you had any luck?'

'I'm afraid not, Inspector.' Miss Leggett turned to the woman on her left. 'We've looked everywhere, haven't we, Pat?' The secretary nodded. 'In all the rooms, including the boiler house and kitchens and Miss Galton has been round the grounds with her dog.'

'I'd like to see Miss Warwick's room myself, please.'

'Very well. You'll take the Inspector, won't you, Pat?'

Newton stood at the door of the bedroom and looked round. It was laid out in exactly the same way as his own; the bed with the built-in alarm clock and radio above it was against one wall, the unit on the other side acted as a dressing-table with chests of drawers at each end and the TV set was beside it on its own stand. The wardrobe, set into the wall, was next to it and by the door was the entrance to the en suite bathroom and lavatory.

'Do you know who's been in here today?'

'Only the maid who reported that the bed hadn't been slept in, Miss Leggett, who came to investigate, and now us.'

'How many master keys are there?'

'Only three. The maid in this section has one, Miss Leggett another and I keep a spare in a locked cabinet in my office.'

Newton went through the contents of the bedroom with minute care and when he had finished, helped Miss Pennington to make up the bed, which he had pulled apart. He stood there for a moment, looking round again; Jane hadn't left a note and the tracksuit, that he had seen her wearing in the gym, and her training shoes were both missing.

'Have you any theories about what

might have happened to her?'

'None at all, I'm afraid. I've no wish to sound unhelpful, sir, but I'm not paid to speculate about our guests. We have a reputation for discretion and confidentiality and any new employee is always told that this must be respected at all times.'

'I take it that that discretion doesn't extend to the people working here.'

'I don't understand what you mean.'

'I've heard a fair amount of gossip about the staff since my arrival — wasn't one of the physiotherapists drowned in the pool recently?'

'That was a tragic accident, sir.'

'And what about that cocaine incident?'

'We do try to screen all the employees here before they start, but no system is perfect.'

'How do you suppose that the police knew where to look for the drugs?'

'Perhaps, sir, they would be the best people to ask.'

Newton went to the window and looked out. 'I take it that the chapel has been searched thoroughly.'

'I did so myself this morning.'

'Why this morning?'

'I always unlock it first thing — some of our guests like to avail themselves of the opportunity for private prayer — and I found that some of the stone-work had come down in the night. I checked to make sure that there was no one inside, locked it up again so that Mr Milroy could inspect it on his return and then told Miss Leggett about it.'

'Is it normally kept locked at night?'

'Oh, yes. Always.'

'Why is that?'

'Someone played a silly practical joke once and the management team here was most anxious that the same thing shouldn't happen again.'

'What was the practical joke?'

'An item of feminine underwear was put on top of the flag-pole, the door to the tower was locked and then the keyhole was filled with chewing gum.'

'Any idea who was responsible?'

'I wouldn't care even to hazard a guess.'

'And you locked it as usual last night?'

'Yes, at dusk.'

'Are you the only one with a key?'

'No, sir. There's a spare in the locked cabinet in my office and Mr Milroy also has one — he likes to play the organ sometimes in the evening.'

'Do you have your key on you?'

'No, sir. It's in my bag in the desk in my office.'

'Would you be kind enough to get it and then perhaps we might meet in the chapel in five minutes.'

'Is there anywhere else you would like to check? If so, I'll bring those keys along as well.'

'Not for the moment, thank you. There is one other thing, though; I don't want anyone to come into this room for the time being and I'd be grateful if you would give instructions to the maid.'

Newton was admiring the stone carving above the door of the chapel when he sensed the presence of something behind him and turned to see Milroy standing a few paces away. The man's hands were tucked into the pockets of his blazer with the exception of his thumbs, which he was moving gently as he looked at the detective with a quizzical smile on his face.

'The chapel falling down and one of our guests missing; curiouser and curiouser. You'll be telling me that you're Lord Peter Wimsey in disguise next.'

'I can hardly believe that a well-informed man like you hasn't heard that nugget of information already.'

'A copper with a sense of humour by all that's marvellous. Yes, I met Pat Pennington a couple of minutes ago; she was actually hurrying, so I knew that something was wrong and she was good enough to tell me all about it in her usual succinct way. Well, I suppose we'd better have a squint at the damage.'

The man took a bunch of keys out of his blazer pocket and Newton watched as he opened the door, then strode across to the metal box on the wall to switch off the burglar alarm.

'Bloody hell! Let him who is without sin cast the first stone.'

Milroy shook his head as they both stood in the nave and looked up towards the clerestory and then down at the oak pews. A three-foot section of the coping had come down, leaving ugly scars on the woodwork where the stones had hit the seats.

'Just as well that no one was in here at the time.'

'It gives me cold shivers just to think about it. Anyone sitting there would have had their skull crushed like an eggshell and there was a service in here only yesterday afternoon.'

'What do you suppose brought it down?'

'Not the foggiest. Might have been the vibration from a low flying aircraft; they sometimes come over here early in the morning — we've even had a few complaints from the guests.'

'It's a wonder it didn't set off the alarm.'

'It's not that type of system; only the doors are wired.'

'Why did you go to the trouble of fitting one? Had any break-ins?'

'No, but some bright spark ran a pair of knickers up the flag-pole, then jammed the lock to the tower. Glover was here at the time and, believe you me, he doesn't find that sort of thing funny and wasn't looking for a repeat performance.'

'Who was responsible?'

'We never found out and, to be honest, we didn't look too far — it might have been one of the guests.'

'When did all this occur?'

'Let's think, now. Yes, it was the spring bank holiday of last year, when Glover came down to open the swimming pool.'

'May I take a look up the tower?'

'What? You don't think that that girl you were minding got in here, do you?'

'It doesn't seem very likely, but if there's one thing I've learned in this business, it's that one covers any eventuality, however unlikely.'

'All right, you're the boss.'

Milroy marched down the aisle and tried the door to the tower.

'Still locked, as you see,' he said, inserting one of the keys on his ring and opening it. 'Let's go up, shall we?'

The two men climbed the spiral staircase and inspected the belfry and its surround, including the observation area at the base of the flag-pole at the top of the tower.

'Well,' said Milroy, 'no sign of the missing mystery girl. If you'll excuse me for a moment, while I'm up here I'd better take a look at that coping; not a task I'm looking forward to all that much — I never did have much of a head for heights.'

Newton stood at the end of the walkway, whilst the other man made his way cautiously along until he reached the damaged section, where he went down on his hands and knees.

'The mortar's rotten,' he shouted back, 'the whole thing's unsafe.'

Milroy began to edge backwards and, at that moment, another stone toppled over the edge and hit the back of one of the pews with an echoing crash, sending a cloud of dust up into the air.

'This is going to cost us a fortune,' he said when he got back. 'There's no doubt in my mind that it would be cheaper to take the whole thing down rather than repair it, but then that would alter its whole character. A clerestory in a church of this size is unusual enough, but the walkway is pretty well unique.'

'Would you mind if I took a look at the other side? I've never come across anything like this before.'

'Go ahead, but you will be careful, won't you? We can't have the Police Federation suing us if you peel off.'

Newton grinned at him. 'Don't worry, I'll be caution personified.'

The detective made his way along the whole length of the walkway on the undamaged side and then, when he got back, the two men descended the staircase and Milroy took him on a conducted tour of the rest of the chapel.

'Do you think I might try the organ?'

'A fellow player, by all that's wonderful! Of course you can, but you will watch the low register, won't you? Too much vibration might bring the 'walls of Jericho' down on us. By the way, what was the condition of the stonework where you were?'

'To be honest, I wasn't paying all that much attention to it, but it seemed in reasonable condition.'

'Good. Right, then, I'll go and switch on the power.'

Newton had been quite an accomplished organist at one time — he had acted as relief for the organ scholar at his college at Oxford on a number of occasions — but he was out of practice and contented himself with one of the simpler Bach cantatas.

'If you stay here much longer,' Milroy said with a loud sigh when the detective had finished, 'I'm going to go into a major decline. Golf and playing the organ are my main hobbies and you knock spots off me at both of them. On top of that, you drive a car I'd give my teeth for.'

'If it's any consolation to you, it's not mine — just lent for the occasion.'

Milroy laughed. 'Thank God for that; at least that piece of good news makes me feel marginally less inadequate.'

'Thanks,' Newton said when they were standing outside, 'I enjoyed playing that instrument enormously.'

'A pleasure. I hope you find that young lady of yours soon. Apart from other considerations, this place can do without any more adverse publicity.'

The detective waited until Milroy had disappeared from view and then walked through the trees and sat on the fence where both Fiona Graham and Jane had climbed over. He lit his pipe and looked towards the chapel; he could just make out the porch and surely, he thought, the light must have come from there. Joe had been quite sure that it was stronger than a torch and there was no way that a car headlight could have been shining from that direction; the chapel was tucked well away from the car park and any of the access roads. Surely, too, masonry falling down on that night of all nights was altogether too much of a coincidence. Even so, he couldn't think why anyone should have been up on the walkway and there had been nothing suspicious about the chapel as a whole, nor in Milroy's attitude; the man had not hesitated to show him anything he wished.

But where the hell had Jane got to? He hadn't failed to notice her blush when she had been talking about Joe; had she gone out to meet him for the same reason as Fiona and had the stable lad been making up stories about mysterious lights? Why was Mrs Hockaday so defensive about him? Was there something in his past that she knew about? The detective shook his head; he felt very directly responsible for his young assistant and the fact that she had wandered out in the night entirely on her own initiative didn't make it any better.

Roger Newton sighed; he was going to need reinforcements to mount a search of the neighbouring countryside and that would mean ringing Kershaw, with all the inevitable complications. He stepped down from the fence and for no reason that he could think of suddenly remembered the barn that Jane had mentioned. Was it too far-fetched to believe that she might have blotted her copy-book with Joe and then decided to lie low for a bit? When he came to consider what he knew of Jane, the very idea seemed absurd, but he nevertheless decided to take a look at it, although fully realising that what he was really doing was putting off the evil hour of admitting defeat to his chief.

It took the detective fifteen minutes to find it and he approached the entrance cautiously, picking his steps with great care to avoid making any noise. He looked inside and up towards the loft, hesitating before going in. He froze suddenly; had it been his imagination or had something moved up there? The sound was not repeated and he crept outside again. The floor of the loft was a good fifteen feet up and the ladder would be bound to be quite heavy, so surely, he reasoned, the place where it was kept couldn't be all that far away. It didn't take him long to find it; there was only one place it could have been, a ditch partially filled with leaves, and confirmation was his discovery of fresh scratch marks in the earth of its base.

'May I come up?' Newton stood in the centre of the barn, looking up towards the entrance to the loft. 'I know you're there, but don't worry, I'm not going to tell anyone else about it.'

There was a long pause and then he caught a glimpse of a face and although he was unable to make out the features, he saw the glint of spectacles.

'Is Jane Warwick up there?'

'Who are you?'

'A detective from Scotland Yard.' He waved his warrant card in her direction. 'Take a look at this if you don't believe me.'

The girl sent down a length of string and Newton tied the card to it.

'Inspector Newton?'

'That's right.'

'Something like this can be forged.'

'Look, Jane Warwick is missing; I haven't got time to play games with you and obstructing the police in their enquiries is a serious offence.'

There was a flurry of activity from above and a short while later, the aluminium ladder descended through the opening and before the girl could start to climb down, the detective began to ascend it.

'I apologise if I've interrupted your snack — please don't stop on my account.'

The young woman flushed and picked up the piece of cake that she had hidden behind one of the packing cases.

'How did you know about this place?'

'Jane told me. Have you any idea what might have happened to her?'

'Search me. She didn't show up for breakfast this morning and when I went to see if she was all right, I found her room locked and there was no reply when I knocked. I asked the chamber maid to open the door in case she had been taken ill and the bed hadn't been slept in.'

'What did you do then?'

'Nothing. I rather assumed that she had spent the night with a bloke.'

'Why did you think that?'

Angela hesitated for a moment, taking another bite out of the piece of chocolate cake. 'She asked me if there was any talent at the riding school.'

'And is there?'

'Good heavens no. There's only Joe Harvey and he's so dim it isn't true. Do you know, he actually told me that there were ghosts walking around the chapel at night! If you ask me, he and my father ought to get together — they'd make a very suitable match for one another.'

'Your father?'

'Yes, he's a bishop and exorcism's his

big thing. I have only ever seen him at it once — the crypt of one of the local churches had been broken into and black masses held in it. You never saw such a performance; I thought he was having an epileptic fit, I mean, he . . . Have I said anything wrong?'

'No, on the contrary, I am greatly indebted to you; you've nudged that thing in my head that's supposed to be a brain.'

'You won't tell Miss Leggett about this place, will you?'

'I wouldn't dream of it. Do I see a bottle of cider over there, by any chance?'

'Yes, would you like some?'

'Would I not? Thirsty weather, this.'

'You're not really an inspector, are you?'

'Scouts' honour.'

'And you were really guarding Jane?'

'In a manner of speaking.'

'Gosh!'

'We've got to find her and quickly. You will keep your ears open, won't you?' Angela nodded eagerly. 'And in the meantime, not a word to a soul about our conversation.'

# 9

'Where's Jane?'

'Arm yourself with a pint, George, and I'll fill you in with what has happened.'

George Wainwright followed his chief to a table in the corner of the saloon bar, sat down and took a long drink from his tankard.

'You may have noticed that young Jane was a bit put out when I gave her nothing further to do.' Wainwright nodded. 'Well, it seems that she had already set up another meeting with Joe Harvey, this time in the middle of the night. She must have left her room wearing much the same sort of clothes as Fiona Graham on the night that she died and I can only assume that she was trying to reconstruct the scene.'

'What did the lad have to say?'

'I was coming to that. He did go out into the field to meet her, but got cold feet, thinking that she was after the same thing as Fiona. He saw her walk back towards the main buildings and then ran away when he saw a light coming from the direction of the chapel. He believes in spooks and ghosts, does Joe, and he was scared silly. Jane hasn't been seen since. I only discovered that she was missing after lunch and a search of the chapel revealed nothing except for the fact that some of the stonework fell down from the gallery during the night. Her bed hadn't been slept in and she hasn't left any message. Any ideas, George?'

Wainwright shook his head. 'It doesn't look good to me at all; want me to sweat it out of this fellow Joe?'

'You think she's gone the same way as Fiona, then?'

'Stands to reason, doesn't it? All that crap about ghosts and lights from the chapel — you'd think he could do better than that. Anyway, I don't need to tell you that blokes like that are always repeating themselves; we'd hardly catch any of them if they didn't.'

'You might have something there, George, but somehow I don't think so.

For one thing, Joe's not exactly the type and there were certainly no signs that he'd been in a struggle — no scratches on his face or anything like that.'

'Perhaps he likes 'em unconscious; you said that other girl was hit on the head, didn't you?' Wainwright saw his chief's grimace of distaste. 'I'm sorry, sir, but you did ask me what I thought.'

'I know I did, George, and you were quite right to bring it up.' Newton looked down at his notes. 'There is one other thing, though. The chapel was kept locked all morning because of that stonework coming down. There's no means of knowing whether it just fell or was pushed, but apart from the fact that the coincidence seems a bit much to swallow, I discovered something else. I found nothing suspicious when Milroy took me round, but then something that that waitress Angela said tickled my subconscious; despite the fact that he said nothing about it and there was no obvious entrance, the place has a crypt.'

'How did you find out about that?'

'A phone call to Pettigrew did the trick

— you remember, he's that retired parson who helps us with the code breaking from time to time; he also compiles crosswords and has far the biggest collection of obscure reference books I've ever seen. The chapel at Croxley Hall features in some tome on English country churches and it definitely has a crypt.'

'And?'

'And, my dear George, I think that another visit there, this time in the fastnesses of the night, might well pay dividends. The crypt may have been sealed up, but if not, methinks our friend Milroy has some explaining to do. By the way, what were you able to dig up on him?'

'Not a great deal, apart from the reason why he resigned his commission. I had a bit of luck and managed to trace his batman, who now works as a commissionaire at one of the big banks. I took him for a drink and he gave me the low-down. According to him, Milroy was always after anything in skirts and succeeded in getting inside the knickers of the Commandant's daughter; he got copped on the job and was invited to resign.'

'Very poetically put, George, and it fits in well enough with what his wife told me. Anything else?'

'No criminal record, but he had the reputation of being on the fiddle; the bloke told me that there was a lot of that sort of thing going on in Germany at that time.'

'And what did he get up to in London?'

'He stayed the night at his club and then took a taxi to an office block in the City.'

'At what time did he leave?'

'About eight-thirty.'

'How did you find all that out?'

'Pretended to be a divorce enquiry agent and slipped a couple of the porters there a little something. Neither of them like him much — said he was a mean bugger.'

'I see. Well, you actually saw him go into the club at about five-thirty on Sunday afternoon and he left again at eight-thirty this morning, but did he stay there the whole time, or did he nip out and return here during the night? That's what I need to know and . . . Ah, here he is.'

'Who?'

'Foxy Mann.'

'That tea-leaf! What do you want with him?'

'He's a reformed character, George; I can vouch for him personally and he's just the bloke to get us into that chapel.'

'Huh!'

The ginger haired ex-burglar was not in the least abashed by the fact that George Wainwright totally ignored his approach.

'Wotcher, mate,' he said, pounding the sergeant so hard on the shoulder that he spilled some of his beer. 'Not losin' any weight, I see.'

Newton saw the flush spreading up Wainwright's neck and steered the man towards the bar.

'What'll you have, Foxy?'

'Tomato juice wiv a dash of Worcestershire.'

'Not on the wagon, are you?'

'Never touch a drop when I'm on the job.' He grinned when he saw the detective's expression. 'Not on that job, either. I used to be friendly wiv a bird, once, in a manner of speakin'; she was on the game and she 'ad a notice on the back of 'er bedroom door: 'Don't stay if you're drunk — you'll only waste my time and your money.' Lot of truth in that.'

'Quite so,' Newton said. 'And you no doubt need a steady hand in your line of country. Any good on medieval locks, Foxy?'

'Lost the key to yer old lady's chastity belt, then, 'ave yer?'

The detective sighed, knowing better than to take the ex-burglar on in the repartee stakes. 'As I told you on the phone, I want to get into this chapel without anyone knowing; there's a mortice and a Yale type lock on the door and an alarm. Think you can do it?'

'Wot's the make?'

'A Brotherton.'

'Don't see why not. It'll be a lot easier now I know that — yer did a good job there, matey.'

Newton gave him a little bow. 'Got all your gear?'

'In me trusty van.'

'You're not still running that dreadful old rattle-trap, are you?'

'Do yer mind? It's me pride an' joy.'

They arrived outside the chapel a few minutes after 1am and while the two detectives kept watch, Foxy made a complete circuit of the building.

'Well, what's the verdict?' Newton asked in a low voice when Foxy got back.

'You 'ave a choice. Either I go up me ladder and take out one of the winders, or I go in through the door and find a key to turn orf the alarm.'

'How much time will you have with that type?'

'Ninety seconds.'

'And your chance of doing so successfully?'

'Knowin' the make and model — ninety per cent.'

'Those odds are good enough for me — it would take hours to deal with one of those windows without damaging it.'

'I beg yours, mate. It would take longer, I grant yer, but not hours.'

'All right, then, on your way, Foxy.'

'OK, but would yer mind withdrawin', 'as the actress said to the bishop'; it puts me orf if people look over me shoulder.'

The two detectives sat on the wooden seat set against the wall of the chapel and rather less than ten minutes later, Foxy Mann reappeared.

'I've fixed both the locks,' he said. 'Now, you've been inside before and know the lay-out; when I open the door, I want yer to go straight to the control box — orl right?'

Foxy Mann handed Newton the powerful torch, sorted out several keys from the bunch he was holding and gave the detective the thumbs-up sign. Although it probably only took the ex-burglar about a minute to switch off the alarm successfully, it seemed a great deal longer and at any moment, Newton was expecting the insistent buzz from the box to be converted into the clamour of the bell set high up on the wall. Foxy's movements seemed impossibly slow and Newton held his breath as the man tried first one key and then another, fiddling with each of them in turn. At the third attempt, the sound was suddenly cut off and the detective exhaled slowly, feeling the tension draining out of him.

'Orl right, mate?'

'Good work, Foxy.'

'I'll just get me bag then and 'ave a gander.'

Wainwright wasn't in the best of humour at having to wait outside again.

'Bloody hell,' he said after half an hour had gone by, 'what the blazes is that bloke getting up to in there? With three of us on the job, we could have checked it out long ago.'

'Patience, George, Foxy'll make a much better job of it on his own; we'd only get in the way and he's sensitive about the possibility of giving away his trade secrets.'

Wainwright stood it with obvious and mounting impatience for another twenty minutes, then got to his feet and began to pace up and down.

'Hold it a moment, George. What's that?'

They both heard the soft humming noise that came from the far side of the building.

'Search me.'

Almost as he spoke, the sound was cut off and total silence descended until a further half hour had passed and Foxy at last reappeared.

'Sorry it took so long, folks. You'd better come an' see wot I've fahnd.'

The ex-burglar locked the door carefully behind them and then fixed a small bell to it with some adhesive.

'Me ears are tuned to it,' he said. 'I don't like the feelin' that some nasty's goin' to creep up behind me — makes me nervous.' He strode across to the stone tomb, which was lying close to the far side of the chapel. ''Ere's the magic bit. The last restin' place of Richard Spense,' he said dramatically, pointing to the inscription on the side, 'or it would 'ave been if someone 'adn't moved the poor sod.' He gripped the far side and pulled up steadily. 'Neat job — nicely 'inged and counter-weighted.' He showed them the row of three plastic buttons, which were set into the stone-work and hidden under the rim when the lid was in place. 'Type of combination lock — that's wot took me most of the time.'

'You wouldn't be showing us all this if she was down there, would you, Foxy?' Newton asked, pointing down the stone steps that led down from the tomb with his torch.

The man shook his head. 'She ain't there, nah, but it looks as if she was; I'll ave to show yer.'

'How did you find it?'

'If yer were right abaht a crypt, there 'ad to be an entrance somewhere and there weren't all that many places to look.' The ex-burglar made a gesture with his hand and they all climbed into the tomb and began to descend the steps. ''Alf a mo while I shut the lid and then, folks, we'll 'ave instant daylight.'

Newton just had time to think that Foxy's American accent was even more excruciating than his English one before the man pressed one of the row of switches at the head of the stairs and the crypt was flooded with light.

'So all the electrics are controlled from inside,' Newton said.

'Not quite. The wirin's connected to

the master switch by the fuse box. That was one of the fings that alerted me — the dust on it's been disturbed.'

The two officers looked round the crypt with its vaulted roof and the long bench set against one of the walls.

'But this is ridiculous,' Wainwright said. 'Why should anyone want to hide the entrance to a place with nothing in it?'

'Because it ain't been empty orl that long and it ain't as empty as it looks.'

'How do you mean?'

'Along this wall, under the bench, we 'ave a row of thirteen-amp sockets an' there's even air conditionin'.' Foxy Mann darted up the steps, pressed down another switch and there was a loud click followed by the hum of an electric motor. 'All mod cons. The fan'll either extract or suck in air — the grill for it's over there.'

'And what makes you think that Jane's been down there?'

'That metal plate.'

Newton went across to the opposite wall and bent down to look at the inscription, reading it aloud with some difficulty, the letters being so worn down as to be almost illegible.

' 'Sacred to the memory of Thomas Neeld,

Who kept his faith and would not yield'.'

The detective straightened up and frowned. 'And what's that got to do with Jane?'

'Although someone 'as taken a lot of care to clean up, you can see the brush marks on the floor, they 'aven't been able to 'ide the fact that someone's been nibblin' at the surround. See 'ere.'

'And?'

'Ullo, ullo, ullo, I said to meself, 'wot 'ave we 'ere?' as the actress said to the bishop.' Foxy selected a rubber-headed hammer from his bag of tools and hit the bottom right hand stud of the four that were holding the plate in position. 'And for me next trick.'

'Christ!' Newton said as the man pushed hard and it slowly pivoted to reveal a dark hole. 'Do you suppose that whoever cleared up also found the opening?'

'Only one way to find aht, mate. Any

volunteers? Don't tell me, stupid question. You've got claustrophobia and your side-kick's too fat.'

He shied away in mock terror as Wainwright clenched his fists, gave them a cheerful grin and disappeared head-first into the tunnel.

'Rather him than me,' Newton said. 'He was closer to the mark than he suspected — I have an absolute horror of dark holes.'

'What the hell is it?' Wainwright asked.

'I imagine that it must have been some sort of escape route for priests and no doubt Thomas Neeld, in particular; families also sometimes used to attend clandestine masses, getting in through entrances like this and, in that case, the tunnel might well go right up to the house.'

'If that's the case, why hasn't Jane turned up?'

Newton raised his shoulders slightly, not wishing to voice his fears and began to prowl around the crypt. All of ten minutes went by before they heard a scraping noise and a very dirty and damp

Foxy emerged backwards from the tunnel. For once, his usual cheerful grin was missing and there was no trace of banter in his voice.

'The bleedin' roof's fallen in.'

★ ★ ★

Jane Warwick wasn't going to risk falling asleep and settled down to watch a late night film on TV until the time she had set to meet Joe. At least, that was her intention, but she was quite incapable of concentrating. Was she taking a stupid risk in going out alone without telling Roger Newton? Suppose she had been wrong about Joe and he was a rapist and a murderer, his story about what had happened between him and Fiona being a pack of lies. And even if what he had told her had been true, might he not take her invitation in the wrong way and try to . . . And what if he did? Joe was undeniably physically attractive and with all the exercise, strict dieting and excitement, she was feeling distinctly and rather urgently . . .

'That's enough of that, Warwick,' she said sternly to herself and switched channels to an earnest discussion on the perils of failing to plan for retirement.

The programme was excrutiatingly boring, but she forced herself to listen to it until ten minutes before she was due to leave. She felt distinctly self-conscious about dressing in the same things as Fiona Graham had been wearing on the night she had died, but as she put on each item, she felt a frisson of guilty excitement as she remembered Joe's description of the way the young physiotherapist had taken them off.

There was no moon, but the sky was clear and the stars brilliant as Jane made her way along the side of the lawn in the shelter of the trees. Would Fiona have used much the same route? It seemed more than likely — surely she wouldn't have run the risk of going out into the open. Once at the stables, Jane hesitated, listening and looking around.

'Joe!' she called softly and then again a little louder, 'Joe!'

The only response was a movement

from inside Snowball's stall, which was not repeated, and then absolute silence. Feeling let down and at the same time in some way relieved, Jane walked out to the field and leaned against the boundary fence, looking back towards the main buildings. Would she have felt like a swim if she had been in Fiona's position? Of course she would — she felt like one now — and she had just started in the direction of the pool, feeling her heart thumping with excitement both at the thought of stripping off and the further reminder of what Fiona and Joe had done on Snowball's back in the field, when she glimpsed something out of the corner of her eye. For one moment she thought she had been mistaken, but then she saw it again — a shaft of light had come from the direction of the chapel.

Jane ran towards it, then, twenty feet short, waited behind the large oak tree within sight of the porch. The chapel door was ajar and after another couple of minutes, when nothing had happened to break the silence, she crept forwards cautiously and looked in. The light was coming from an open tomb standing by the far wall and she tip-toed across to it and peered in. The steps leading down were a temptation she was unable to resist and she climbed in, stopping in amazement at the bottom of the flight of stairs when she saw the crypt under the brilliant strip lighting.

Jane just had time to take in the long bench with the microscope, the grinding wheel, polisher and the neat row of instruments and had just picked up the largest piece of a collection of jewellery set out on a baize cloth, when there was a loud thud from above and she felt a blast of air against her ear drums. A second or two went by before she reacted and then she dashed back up the stairs and pushed up against the lid of the tomb. She just had time to take in the fact that it was absolutely unyielding when the light suddenly went out.

Jane had never been in total blackness before, not the sort of blackness where there wasn't even the merest chink of light, and she found it utterly terrifying. She located the row of switches at the top of the stairs and flicked them all up and down, knowing that it would be hopeless and yet feeling a compulsion to try. On several occasions, she tried to sit on the top step and push up with her feet, but it was too narrow, she was unable to apply any real pressure and, after she had slipped on one occasion, falling down three steps and landing painfully, she gave it up.

Jane lost count of the number of times she barked herself against the stone walls as she forced herself to make a complete circuit of the crypt and when she had finished, she sat on the chair by the bench and leaned backwards, refusing to give way to the tears which were threatening to break through. She had already tried shouting, but the way the sound came back at her was enough for her to know that it would prove to be a complete waste of time, certainly until someone came in to clean the chapel in the morning, provided, of course, that was done regularly. Already, she was finding that one of the worst things was the fact that she had no idea of the time — her watch didn't have a luminous dial — and there was also the ever-present fear of what was going to happen to her. She hadn't the slightest doubt that Fiona, too, had stumbled on what was going on in the chapel and if the people responsible had been ruthless enough to kill her, then . . .

With every passing minute, the blackness seemed to press in on her more and more and when she was near to screaming point, she went back up the steps and pounded on the under surface of the lid of the tomb as hard as she could with the legs of the chair. It was as futile as she knew it would be and more to prevent herself from losing control than for any other reason, she decided to make one last circuit of the walls.

This time, she came across something she had missed the first time round, a metal plate set into the wall on the side opposite to the bench. Why was it there? There were large metal studs standing out from each of the four corners and when she ran her fingers all round the edge, there seemed to be a minute crack between it and the surrounding stone. Could it possibly be something to do with a ventilation system? It didn't seem at all likely, even though there obviously was one — the air in the crypt was quite fresh — but doing something, anything, was better than sitting there getting more and more anxious.

Jane felt around the bench, selected a pair of forceps and began to pick at the mortar around the plate, which seemed softer than elsewhere. She kept it up for a good half hour, but then her fingers began to get sore, one of the blades snapped off and she was unable to delude herself any longer. It had been a stupid idea, the thing was obviously a memorial plaque to someone or other and she had been wasting her time. Jane drew back her foot and gave the metal rectangle a hefty blow with the sole of her tennis shoe. At first, she thought she had imagined that the plaque had given a fraction, but when she felt around the edge with the tips of her fingers, she was no longer left in any doubt. She pounded away until her foot was bruised and sore, the steady progress she was making spurring her on, and eventually the metal plate and the semi-circular stone to which it was attached, rotated, leaving a space large enough for her to climb through.

After she had explored the first few feet of the tunnel, Jane sat down on the floor with her back to the wall, wondering if she would be able to find the courage to crawl along it. It obviously hadn't been opened for years and equally clearly wasn't a ventilator shaft — the air coming out of it was stale and damp — and the thought of getting stuck in it filled her with horror. And what if it was merely a priest hole and someone were to come back into the crypt and shut her up inside? She got up again and began to work the stone steadily backwards and forwards; with every movement, it seemed to rotate more easily on its spindle and at least, she thought, there was a metal handle set into the inner surface, which should, she thought, enable her to open it from the inside. Where would the tunnel lead? Back to the house? Would the people who had shut her in know about it and if they did, would they be waiting for her at the other end?

Half an hour or so later — it could easily have been longer — Jane was still trying to come to a decision, fear of the unknown being greater than that of the crypt. She had tried to block the stairway using the chair and some of the equipment from the bench in order to give herself at least some time if they decided to come for her, but by now, she was beginning to wonder if they had settled for starving her to death. Quite suddenly, she felt a current of air against her cheek and she rose to her feet, the goose pimples standing out all over her body. There was the merest hint of a break in the darkness coming from the direction of the top of the stairs and then, almost simultaneously, she heard the crash of breaking glass and the thud of the lid of the tomb being slammed shut again. As soon as the spiritous smell reached her, Jane dived through the opening in the wall, not pausing to think and, reaching behind her, pulled hard on the metal handle. The heavy stone moved much more easily than she had been expecting, she heard a loud click and when she tried to reopen it, found it stuck fast. With the greatest difficulty, she twisted round and felt all over the inner surface, but after ten minutes frustrating effort and with the sweat pouring off her, she still hadn't found a way of moving it. Jane lay on the damp floor of the tunnel and began to shake all over, feeling the hysteria rising up inside her. She gritted her teeth, riding the moment out, and then began to crawl along the underground passage.

When she was about thirty feet along it, Jane had a rest. Now that the initial shock had worn off, she gave herself a severe telling off; against all the odds, she had managed to get out of the crypt, the tunnel had obviously been an escape route in the past and even if it was partially blocked, there was no reason why she shouldn't be able to burrow her way out. At least, too, the air was breathable and there was no trace of the ether, or whatever chemical it was that had been thrown into the crypt.

For the next few yards, the going was relatively easy, the passage being lined with bricks, and even though in places sections of the roof had given way, she was able to crawl past without undue difficulty. Although it was pitch black and she had become almost completely disorientated, she had the strong impression that she was descending slightly and this was confirmed when she felt the water soaking the elbows and knees of her tracksuit. It was only an inch or two deep and she continued through it and shortly afterwards began to edge her way up a steady incline.

The tunnel gradually became narrower and for the first time she began to have to dig her way through, shifting the damp earth back with her hands. Very soon after, Jane came to a point where virtually all the bricks had fallen in and she had just wriggled her shoulders through a particularly narrow section, when something soft and damp landed on the bare skin of her back where her tracksuit had ridden up. Jane gave an involuntary jerk, there was a momentary silence and then a large piece of the roof came down with a dull thud, burying her in earth from the shoulders down. She tried to crawl forwards, but every movement, even the slightest, provoked yet another fall and, in any case, she was wedged solidly. The wet clinging soil was everywhere, in her hair, her ears, and she could even feel it gritting between her teeth; Jane rested her head on her hands and gave in to despair.

\* \* \*

'How bad is it, Foxy?'

'Abaht as bad as it could be. The tunnel's completely blocked fifty or so feet along. I did try to start diggin', but all that did was bring dahn more of the roof.'

'Are you quite sure that Jane's in there? That fall might have happened ages ago.'

''Ave a gander at this.'

He showed them the white-painted piece of metal about quarter of an inch long, holding it up between his forefinger and thumb.

'The metal tag off a shoe lace?'

'You got it. And you did say she was

wearin' trainers?'

'I'm afraid so. What do you suggest next?'

' 'Alf a mo, mate — I've got to put me thinkin' cap on. It don't pay to rush things.'

Foxy Mann paced around for a few minutes and then took a sheaf of metal rods out of his bag, each section about two feet long and no thicker than a pencil.

'I'm going' to screw two or three of these togevver and then stick a couple of 'em through the roof; that should give us the direction of the tunnel and some idea of its depth.'

'All right, Foxy, you're in charge.'

Newton kept telling himself that what had happened was in no way his fault, but he still felt responsible for Jane. She had shown herself to be hard-working and resourceful with a real flair for the job, but tough and resilient though she seemed to be, she had been in the tunnel for twenty-four hours already and even if she was still alive, it didn't take the exercise of much imagination to guess what sort of condition she must be in. The detective tried to get it out of his mind by trying to work out what could possibly have been going on in the crypt, but it proved to be a futile task and by the time that Foxy had reappeared, he had got precisely nowhere.

'Right,' the ex-burglar said when he had climbed out of the tunnel, 'let's clear up in 'ere and then we'll be orf — I can pull up me rods from outside.'

Foxy Mann swept up the earth from the floor of the crypt and when he had thrown it into the passage, closed the stone door; he then had one last look round and when he was satisfied that there was no trace of them having been down there, gathered up all his tools and went up the stairs last, shutting the tomb and locking it.

'You won't take it wrong if I ask you to keep watch again, will you? The roof of the tunnel's so unstable that we can't afford to tramp arahnd too much.'

The churchyard was surrounded by a stone wall and the two detectives sat on it, watching the shadowy figure of Foxy

Mann and the beam of his torch as it picked out some of the gravestones.

'I reckon I've fahnd the exit to the tunnel,' he said, when he got back. 'The line of it leads straight towards the big 'eadstone over there and even though I can't make aht all the letters, I fink it's our friend Tommy Neeld again. I've also worked aht where the roof's given way, but I reckon there ain't been much of a fall cos there ain't a depression in the grahnd.'

'Any sign of the gravestone having been moved?'

'Nah, and it would 'ave been obvious. I reckon me jemmy'll shift it, though.'

Newton walked across the grass and bent down to take a look himself. As Foxy had said, the head-stone, which was standing drunkenly at an angle, was so weathered and covered with lichen that most of the lettering was indecipherable but, with the eye of faith, the detective was able to make out enough to confirm what the burglar had suggested. Foxy went down on his knees, ran a long-bladed knife along the side of the horizontal slab set into the turf and after a minute or two gave a grunt of satisfaction.

'It's lyin' on a brick surround,' he said. 'I'll just prise it up, put a wedge in and then we're in business. Come on, superman, lend a hand.'

Wainwright squatted down, put his hands under the stone and keeping his back straight, slowly straightened up, grunting with the effort, until the stone was on its side. Foxy Mann shone his torch into the dark, brick-lined hole that was revealed and pointed to the metal rungs.

'All mod cons,' he whispered. 'Do you see, the tunnel goes in both directions, that way to the chapel and the other towards the 'ouse. This must 'ave been an air vent and an alternative way aht.'

He gave the two detectives a cheerful thumbs-up sign and then disappeared from view along the limb of the tunnel leading towards the chapel. At first, he thought that the girl was dead; he could just make out the dark hair on the top of her head, which was resting on her hands, but then, when he was only three feet away, he saw a minute movement. Even that was enough to bring another sprinkling of earth down and he crept forward, scraping some of it away with infinite care and patience and moving her hair to one side.

'Ullo, mate,' he said, as she opened one eye, ''ow're you doin'? Still alive and kickin'?'

'Just about.'

He only just caught her hoarse whisper and gave her fingers a gentle squeeze.

'Look, luv, your mates are upstairs — I'm just the 'ired 'and — and we may 'ave to dig you aht. We'll be as quick as we can, but it's bahnd to take a minute or two. I'm just going' back up for 'alf a mo, but I'll leave you the torch. Orl right?' Her nod was almost imperceptible, but even so another dusting of earth came down on to her head. 'That's the ticket.'

Moving only inches at a time, Foxy inspected the roof above her head for several minutes, measuring the dimensions of the tunnel at that point with the piece of string from his pocket, and then crawled back to the entrance.

'It's goin' to be pretty tricky,' he said, when he had explained to the two detectives that Jane was all but completely buried. 'I take it that you don't want them nasties to know that we've got 'er aht.'

'I'd certainly prefer it that way, but obviously not to the extent of slowing things up too much, or, most importantly, of adding to the risk.'

'Right. Well, as a start, I'm goin' to 'ave to shore up the tunnel over 'er 'ead; the roof's OK until abaht a foot short of 'er and then it's just bare earth, which comes dahn if you speak above a whisper.'

'How are you going to do that?'

'Any dustbins arahnd 'ere?'

'I'm pretty sure I saw some behind the kitchens.'

Foxy Mann nodded. 'See if you can find a metal one and I'll get me wire cutters from the van. If I take the bottom off, I reckon it should just abaht go dahn there and if I slip it over 'er 'ead and shoulders, she should be safe while we decide what to do.'

'I think I'll go down and keep her

company while you and George get things ready. OK, Foxy?'

'It's a nice idea, mate, but the fewer people who go dahn there the better.'

'You're the boss.'

It took them an hour to get Jane out, but eventually they achieved it without having to dig down from above. Once the dustbin was in place, Foxy was able to scrape most of the earth away from around her head and shoulders and by dint of wriggling from side to side and with the additional help of a steady pull on her outstretched arms, Jane was at last able to get free from the clinging embrace of the earth.

'George,' Newton said, when they had got her to the surface, 'would you carry her to the car? We must get her to hospital as soon as possible.'

'What I'd really like is a hot bath and something to drink.'

'Of course you would. Your room's locked up, but you can use mine.'

'I've got the key in my pocket — at least I think I have.'

Her attempt at a smile reassured him

further. 'Just the ticket. Right, George, I'll lead the way, shall I?'

When Wainwright got back, dawn was just beginning to break and he helped Foxy Mann to replace the gravestone.

'They might see that we've been 'ere, but let's 'ope not,' the ex-burglar said, when he had filled in the cracks around it with some bits of moss.

Wainwright rubbed some of the earth off his hands. 'They won't unless they've got someone like you on their books. I never thought I'd say this, Foxy, but you're a bloody marvel.'

'It's not me you should be talking abaht, mate, it's that girl of yours. Can you imagine lyin' in a dark tunnel for twenty-four 'ours, wet through and unable to move a muscle in case you smuvver yourself and still come up smilin'? There's yer bloody marvel.'

# 10

'Need any help?'

Jane sat on the lavatory seat and could only nod her head as reaction suddenly hit her and her teeth began to chatter.

'Right. Let's get those things of yours off first.'

She didn't have time to feel embarrassed as he helped her into the bath, stripped off her clothes and began to direct the water from the shower attachment all over her body, washing away the mud and grime. An hour later, hair shampooed, tingling pleasantly and in a clean nightdress, she smiled at Roger Newton as he came out of the bathroom, having cleaned up.

'I don't have to go to hospital, do I?'

The detective looked at her doubtfully. 'Well, I am particularly anxious that the opposition doesn't get to know that we've been able to rescue you, but, on the other hand, I suppose you would be perfectly safe right here; I have given strict instructions that no one is to come in and you would be able to secure the door from the inside. We wouldn't be able to find anyone to sit with you, though, at least not for some time.'

'I'll be perfectly all right on my own, really. I couldn't bear a lot of fuss and I hate hospitals.'

Newton glanced at his watch and made up his mind. 'One or two people will be about by now and perhaps it would be best if you stayed put. Would you like me to get you a sleeping pill? I have a few in my bedroom.'

'No, thank you.'

'Well, you most certainly must have something to eat, although I'm sure it would be wise to go easy to start with. How about some cold milk and a little scrambled egg?'

'Funnily enough, I'm not at all hungry — past it, I suppose — but what you suggest would be lovely. How will you get it, though? They don't provide a room service.'

'I expect they'll make an exception if I

ask them nicely.' He lifted up the telephone. 'Miss Leggett, please.' There was a long pause. 'Ah, good morning, Inspector Newton here. I would like breakfast brought to Miss Warwick's room, please . . . Yes, right away. Cold milk, orange juice, bran flakes, scrambled eggs, toast and coffee for two . . . Yes, two. The fingerprint expert is here and I thought that you would prefer that your guests didn't know what was going on; that's why I would like you to bring it personally and not the maid.'

The detective noted with some anxiety that Jane ate practically nothing, but at least she drank both the glasses of milk and some of the orange and, although pale and drawn, seemed cheerful enough.

'Do you feel strong enough to tell me what happened?'

She nodded, giving him a full account of everything that had occurred and he listened without interrupting; then, in his turn, described how they had managed to find her.

'What are you going to do next?'

'I think that a visit to the Bishop's palace would be in order while you get some beauty sleep.'

Newton was fully expecting to find Jane out to the world and not answering his knock when he came back in the late afternoon, but not only did she open the door straight away, but was fully dressed.

'Couldn't you get off to sleep?'

'I dozed for a bit, but then I watched the cricket on TV.'

The detective looked at her anxiously, still not happy that he had made the right decision in letting her stay alone in the room, but at least she had eaten the bran flakes and although, most unlike her, she didn't say much, she did listen with concentration while he told her about his visit to the Bishop.

'After meeting him, I'm quite ready to believe what your friend Angela told you about him — he's a perfectly dreadful man who looks as if he's got a slice of lemon permanently in his mouth. Anyway, the tiara and the rest of his wife's most valuable pieces of jewellery were stolen.'

'While he was here?'

'Could be, but he doesn't know for certain.'

'Why ever not?'

'She last used it for a posh reception about a month before their visit and it was only several weeks later, some time after their return, when she wanted another piece, that they discovered the robbery. The safe, which only has two keys, one that the Bishop always keeps with him and the other that his solicitor looks after, hadn't been tampered with and there is no record of the burglar alarm having gone off — it's connected to the local police station.'

'So it's quite on the cards that his keys were nicked while he was here?'

'That's right.'

'Who's your bet? Milroy?'

'Well, he was the one responsible for getting the chapel refurbished and he does go in for expensive suits and may well have set Ruth up in her flat, but he was in London last Sunday night; at least he did attend that meeting with the Treasurer of this place yesterday morning. Interestingly enough, he was also up in Town on the night that Fiona Graham was killed — he goes up regularly on the third Sunday of every month. I was proposing to check on his alibi tomorrow.'

'Do you think I might do that? I was hoping to see my uncle tomorrow anyway.'

'That's not such a bad idea — I'm quite sure you wouldn't want to stay cooped up here any longer. We'll smuggle you out when it gets dark.'

'Would you let me have Foxy's phone number in London? I'd like to thank him personally.'

'Can do.'

★ ★ ★

'Wot? You wonder woman, or somefink?'

Jane laughed as Foxy Mann did a double take as she came up to him at the bar and introduced herself.

'You're havin' me on — it can't be.'

'I must have looked like something the cat brought in.'

'You can say that again, mate, but if I'd known wot you were really like, I'd never 'ave let the 'orrible 'ulk carry you orf like that.'

Chatting to Foxy for half an hour did Jane all the good in the world. He flirted outrageously with her and told her scurrilous stories and unlikely tales of amorous adventures that had her weak with laughter.

'I really am grateful, Foxy,' she said as they got up to leave, 'not only for the other night, but for just now as well.'

'Only too 'appy to oblige. Any uvver time — just say the word.'

'Do you really mean that?'

'Straight up, 'as the bishop said to the actress'.'

'Well, there was one thing; I was planning to interview a girl to do with this business in her flat later this afternoon and I have a hunch — and it's no more than that — that she may have some drugs hidden there. If so, it would give me just the lever I need.'

'An' you want yours truly to 'ave a look-see?'

'I know it's asking a lot, but . . . '

'Not anuvver word, princess. Lead me to it.'

Jane's guess proved correct; after Foxy

had dealt with the lock of the door to the flat in what seemed only a matter of seconds, she kept guard while he went inside. The man reappeared some ten minutes later and showed her the elaborately decorated tin labelled 'china tea'.

'It's in 'ere.'

Jane opened the box and took a cautious sniff. 'Good work, Foxy.'

'Would you like to show me where it was?'

'Yes, please.'

When the ex-burglar had returned the tin to its place in a wall cupboard in the kitchen, he made a gesture towards the half-open door of the bedroom.

'It's sort of cozy in there — you wouldn't fancy a bit of 'ow's your father, would you?'

'Not when I'm on duty, Foxy.'

The man gave her a cheerful grin. 'You didn't mind me askin'?'

'I was flattered.'

'Anuvver time, perhaps?'

Jane rang Roger Newton at Croxley Hall to get his approval for what she had in mind and soon after five she was waiting in the corridor outside the flat with one of the detective constables attached to her section when Ruth Lavington came out of the lift a few minutes after five-thirty. The young woman was carrying a cardboard box full of groceries and Jane selected the moment when she had put it down and had just put the key in the door.

'Here,' she said, 'let me help you.'

From the expression on her face, it was obvious that she had half-recognised the detective, but couldn't quite place her, but although obviously uneasy, she thanked her and made way for her to go in. Jane put the box down on the chair in the hall and took her warrant card out of her bag.

'I'm sorry to walk in on you like this, but I have something important to discuss with you.'

Ruth Lavington took one look over Jane's shoulder, saw the constable who was standing at the door and her whole body drooped slightly.

'You'd better come in here.' She led the

way into the living-room and then turned to face the detective. 'Well?'

'I'm investigating the murder of a physiotherapist at Croxley Hall and I think you knew her.'

'I did and I heard that she drowned accidentally. Anyway, what's it to do with me? I haven't been there for months.'

'She was killed because she went out in the night to meet a boy and found a light on in the chapel on her way back. It was coming from the crypt, which had been fitted out as a workshop to reset stolen jewellery. Last Sunday night, I was shut up in there myself and the same thing very nearly happened to me — I was very lucky to get out alive. Derek Milroy was responsible for getting the chapel done up, wasn't he, and although he claims to have very little money, how come he wears expensive suits, has a set of fancy golf clubs and set you up here?'

'He didn't set me up here, as you put it, and anyway he couldn't possibly have had anything to do with what happened to you.'

'How can you be so sure?'

'He was here with me for the whole of Saturday night.'

'He might have crept out while you were asleep.'

Ruth Lavington flushed slightly. 'I recognise you now and I bet you had a snoop round my bedroom, so I might as well tell you that Derek couldn't have gone anywhere unless I'd untied him and I didn't.'

'Was he also here on the night that Fiona was murdered?'

'Yes, if it was the third Sunday of the month — he always comes here then.'

'If he didn't put you into this flat, who did?'

'Look, I've already told you as much as . . .'

'I'd much rather continue our chat here, but we could always search your flat, you know. We don't need a warrant for drug cases and if you'd prefer to come down to the station, I'm . . .'

'All right, you don't need to spell it out.' The young woman sighed. 'It was Mr Glover, if you must know. He thought I had been harshly treated and he gave it to me as compensation for pleading guilty and keeping Croxley Hall out of the news; he also found me that job with one of his companies.'

'That was generous of him.'

Ruth Lavington suddenly rose to her feet, her eyes blazing. 'I've had enough of this. You get into my flat under false pretences, you make unpleasant insinuations about someone who has only tried to help me, you accuse my friend of something he hasn't done and then you threaten me. Get out.'

The adrenalin had stopped pumping by the time that Jane had reached her uncle's club; she was only too well aware that she hadn't handled the interview with Ruth Lavington at all well and the preceding couple of days were also catching up with her fast. She had completely lost her appetite and had the greatest difficulty in finishing the poached turbot, which was the blandest item on the menu.

'Look, I didn't mean you to take me quite so seriously,' her uncle said as he looked at her with concern across the table when she was toying with a sorbet.

'You must have lost a good stone since I last saw you and you look distinctly peaky.'

'I've had rather a rough couple of days.'

'Sorry to hear that — found your murderer yet?'

'Yes, I think so, but it's not going to be easy to prove.'

'Tell me about it. No, on second thoughts, not just for the moment.' He beckoned to the head waiter. 'Parker, is the Fytton room free?'

'Yes, Sir Henry.'

'Bring us our coffee in there, would you and I'd be grateful if you'd make quite sure that we're not disturbed.'

He took her into the room, waited until the man had gone and then locked the door behind him.

'Now, young Jane, what's been going on?'

The control, which she had been struggling to maintain throughout the meal, suddenly snapped.

'Oh, Uncle Henry . . .'

He had the instinct not to say anything, just hugging her tightly until the storm had blown itself out and she was able to tell him about the horror of being entombed in the damp blackness of the tunnel.

'I'm all right now,' she said at the end of it. 'Thank you for being so understanding.'

He gripped her hand a little more tightly. 'One does need to be able to let go after an experience like that, I wish I had had the . . . '

'Wish you'd had what?'

'Never mind — it was a long time ago. Now, I have some rather interesting information for you.'

★ ★ ★

'Good morning,' Newton said briskly, as he came into the main administration offices at Croxley Hall. 'Good of you all to have come along. As the senior staff here, I thought you would like me to let you know how we were getting on in our search for Jane Warwick. Do sit down everybody.'

Newton took the chair behind the desk

and watched with interest as Milroy settled himself comfortably in the one easy chair and crossed his legs, flicking a speck of dust from his immaculate slacks.

'Firstly,' Newton continued, 'may I introduce Sergeant Wainwright to you all. George, on my far left is Miss Galton, the superintendent physiotherapist, next to her Mr Milroy, the estate manager, Miss Leggett, the domestic supervisor and acting senior administrator, and Miss Pennington, the secretary.'

Wainwright nodded to each of them in turn and sat down himself next to the door, notebook in hand.

'Everyone comfortable?' Newton asked. 'Splendid. Well, first of all, I had better explain about Jane Warwick and why her disappearance has caused us particular concern. The fact is that she is a member of our staff — one of our young detective constables.'

Newton had been expecting some reaction, if not to create a sensation, but he was disappointed; none of the four in front of him moved or changed their facial expression.

'Why did we both come here in the first place?' the detective went on. 'The answer is quite simple — Mr Graham called us in because he wasn't at all happy about the circumstances of his daughter's death. Why not? Let me remind you what happened. Almost exactly two months ago, Fiona, a rather high-spirited young lady, left her room in the middle of the night to meet Joe Harvey. Nothing all that strange about that, you might say; he's an attractive young man and a girl like her wasn't the sort to let the grass grow under her feet. After she had left him, though, she saw a light coming from the direction of the chapel, went to investigate and the following morning was found dead in the swimming pool by Miss Galton. She wasn't drowned accidentally, she was murdered.'

'That's nonsense. There was an inquest and . . . '

Newton fixed Miss Leggett with an icy stare and the woman's voice trailed off.

'You didn't like Fiona at all and she did play several rather nasty tricks on you, didn't she?'

'Are you trying to suggest that I had something to do with Fiona's death?'

'What I am suggesting will, I hope, become clear in a moment. Several other curious things have happened here, starting with the finding of cocaine in Ruth Lavington's room. There is someone here who rather enjoys snooping around the staff quarters and, it seems, sending anonymous letters to the police. Miss Galton was an obvious candidate for the post of administrator and that affair can't have done her cause much good.'

Newton watched as Miss Leggett, who, up to that moment, had been sitting as if starched, suddenly seemed to crumple under the concentrated stare of the Superintendent Physiotherapist.

'Having discovered that Fiona had last been seen going towards the chapel, Jane Warwick decided to set up a reconstruction last Sunday. Joe was there again, saw a light as before and, being frightened of ghosts, ran off. With Jane's disappearance, the answer seemed likely to be in the chapel and Mr Milroy was good enough to show me round. What he didn't show me, though, was the crypt; not a musty crypt that had been bricked-up centuries ago, but one equipped with lighting and ventilation and which has a cunningly concealed entrance through a tomb. Now, you were responsible for refurbishing the chapel, weren't you Mr Milroy?'

'Yes, but I knew nothing about a crypt and anyway . . . '

'You couldn't have had anything to do with Fiona's death or Jane's disappearance, could you? Why not? Because on both occasions you were tied up, quite literally, I believe, in London.'

Milroy, who had been listening to the detective with an expression of cynical amusement on his face, straightened up and Newton saw his knuckles turn white as he gripped the arms of the easy chair.

'What was the crypt being used for? If I tell you that it was a workshop for the resetting of stolen jewellery, which was delivered on those Sunday nights when Mr Milroy was in London, would you believe me? Probably not, but it's a fact. Jane Warwick saw the light in the chapel and went to investigate. It really was very careless of whoever left the tomb open, particularly when something similar had happened with Fiona, but perhaps it wasn't just carelessness. Was Jane seen going in the direction of the paddock and was it felt wise to deal with her? Be that as it may, she went down into the crypt, was shut in, the lights were put out and some time later, a bottle, probably of ether, was thrown in. I don't doubt that after a suitable interval the extractor fan was turned on and the person responsible went down to clear up and remove the body. Ruth Lavington is a skilled art worker and most versatile, I understand; is resetting precious stones one of her many talents?'

Newton paused and looked directly at Milroy, who stared back, the sweat standing out in beads on his forehead.

'Another problem,' the detective went on, 'was the fact that Miss Galton had recently had the idea of writing a history of the chapel. That must have caused consternation in the ranks when our murderer heard about it. A conscientious person like Miss Galton wouldn't have had to do much research work to discover the existence of a crypt and that might well have been the end of a very profitable venture. What better way was there of solving the difficulty than to send an anonymous letter to Mr Glover, particularly when there was someone else waiting in the wings to take over as administrator, someone whom they thought to be both stupid and incompetent.'

Miss Leggett had gone purple in the face, but Newton ignored her completely.

'I mentioned stolen jewellery; well, I have been doing a little homework and although robbery these days is hardly all that rare an occurrence, it is surely stretching coincidence a bit far to find that so many people had had their houses robbed while staying here. What put us on to that was the fact that the tiara belonging to Angela Westmoreland's mother, the Bishop's wife, was seen in the crypt and the thieves must have used keys to open both the house and the safe. The Bishop is quite sure that he had his keys with him here — he is never parted from them

— and who checks the rooms regularly and could have had impressions made of them?'

Everyone turned to look at Miss Leggett, who stared back, a wild expression on her face.

'Yes, I thought the same at first, but there is someone else who had just the same opportunities. Who was so kind to Angela Westmoreland, even asking her to tea in her room when she was obviously homesick, that the girl told her all about her home circumstances and even showed her the picture of her mother wearing the tiara? Who was the only person here to whom Miss Galton spoke about her chapel project? Why, none other than everyone's confidante, the self-effacing and unambitious Patricia Pennington, who was here before anyone else, who has all the keys in her office and who made sure that no one else went into the chapel that morning until the crypt had been cleared, by knocking down . . . '

The secretary, who, up to that moment, had been sitting so quietly that the others had hardly noticed her presence, made a sudden dash for the second door, which led to the ante-room, and had been left ajar. Before anyone else had time to move, she reached it and wrenched it fully open; Jane Warwick was standing there in her tracksuit and when she took a step forward, the woman recoiled and let out a cry of terror.

# 11

'You're not trying to tell me that a woman like that had the crypt of that chapel made into a workshop, organised a series of robberies and murdered Fiona, all on her own, are you?'

The big Australian threw the long typewritten report that he had just finished studying on to Roger Newton's desk and looked up aggressively.

'Certainly not. She was just the technician who reset the stones and supplied information about the guests and occasionally their keys. I think it very unlikely that she was the one who killed Fiona.'

'Who did, then?'

'That crypt must have cost a lot of money and a good deal of expertise to convert and it was not done by the contractors who were responsible for the rest of the work. Who, do you suppose, would have had the money and resources to have had it done on the quiet and who would have been able to terrorise Miss Pennington so efficiently that she's still refusing to say a thing?'

'Glover!'

'You know a great deal more about our friend Glover than you let on, don't you, Mr Graham, and he wasn't called Glover in those days, was he? Let me remind you. A certain young Australian soldier was in a Japanese prisoner of war camp in Malaya in 1944. Every time one of the prisoners came into contact with a guard, he had to bow and, one day, after a monkey had got into the compound and was sitting on top of one of the huts, the young Australian decided to demonstrate his contempt for the Japs by showing that same mark of respect to our simian friend. The Commandant was not amused and it would have meant a flogging, or worse, had it not been for a certain British soldier in the camp, who was not averse to obtaining privileges by selling himself to those guards who were interested. The Commandant was rumoured to be that way inclined himself and so it proved; a deal was struck and you got off with a week in one of those cages. Bad enough, but nothing like so bad as it might have been.

'You were torn by the situation; in one way deeply grateful, in another you were revolted. Anyway, later on I imagine that it was all water under the bridge, you may have become more tolerant and perhaps you reasoned that the man might have changed. On top of that, he now had a different name and had been very successful and perhaps it also crossed your mind that someone like him, who would certainly not pose any sexual threat to Fiona, might be just the person to keep an eye on her.'

Graham nodded his head. 'You're quite correct and I should have told you right at the beginning, but, on the other hand, I had done some homework of my own on Glover and it was clear to me that if his past had leaked out, it would clearly have done him a power of no good. And after all, as you said, I did owe him a real debt of gratitude. What are you proposing to do about him?'

'I doubt if there's anything we will be able to do. That Pennington woman is clearly not going to talk, I can't believe that he hasn't covered his tracks and he will no doubt claim that a gang organised it all without his knowledge.'

'But you don't believe that yourself?'

'Not for a minute; not only are the fraud squad interested in Glover, even though they haven't been able to prove anything either, but I just don't believe that he would have set up Ruth Lavington in the way he did and kept Milroy sweet by providing him with fancy suits just to protect himself from adverse publicity. No, he wanted to prevent any interest in the place developing at all and, don't forget, he had also decided to move Miss Galton.'

'Yes, I was forgetting that. Tell me, how did you manage to get to the bottom of it?'

'Largely thanks to Jane, here, and the fact that luckily the Pennington woman cracked when I set up that little confrontation.'

Graham nodded again and his lips set

into a hard line. 'I have to admit that when I first came here I thought that you were too smooth by half and that Miss Warwick was just there for decoration. I'd just like you to know that I couldn't have been more wrong — you've both done an excellent job, particularly you, young lady, and I'll be letting your superiors know about it.'

★ ★ ★

'Have you seen this?'

Roger Newton took the newspaper from Jane Warwick and let out a low whistle after he had read the short piece on the front page.

'MP KILLED IN MOTORWAY CRASH' the headline proclaimed and underneath: 'MP and successful businessman, Mr Leonard Glover, was killed instantly last night, when his car collided with the arch of a bridge on the M4 last night. Mr Glover, who was unmarried, was alone in the vehicle at the time and a police spokesman said that the car, which appeared to have been travelling at high speed, was so badly damaged that it was doubtful if it would be possible to say whether or not there had been a mechanical failure. An obituary appears on page 8.'

'Suicide?'

'Seems more than likely,' Newton replied.

'But why?'

'I can think of only two people who might know the answer to that and I don't see either of them being prepared to talk about it.'

'Two people? I can imagine Graham refusing to accept that Glover had got away with it and threatening to expose him publicly, even if the evidence wasn't absolutely cast iron, but who's the second?'

Newton gave the heavy glass ashtray a smart blow with the bowl of his pipe. 'There are some people in the security service who seem to know a remarkable amount about Glover and they're not bound by quite the same rules as us. What did you say your Uncle Henry did in Whitehall?'

We do hope that you have enjoyed reading this large print book.

Did you know that all of our titles are available for purchase?

We publish a wide range of high quality large print books including:
**Romances, Mysteries, Classics
General Fiction
Non Fiction and Westerns**

Special interest titles available in large print are:
**The Little Oxford Dictionary
Music Book, Song Book
Hymn Book, Service Book**

Also available from us courtesy of Oxford University Press:
**Young Readers' Dictionary
(large print edition)
Young Readers' Thesaurus
(large print edition)**

For further information or a free brochure, please contact us at:
**Ulverscroft Large Print Books Ltd.,
The Green, Bradgate Road, Anstey,
Leicester, LE7 7FU, England.
Tel:** (00 44) **0116 236 4325**
**Fax:** (00 44) **0116 234 0205**

*Other titles in the
Linford Mystery Library:*

# TO LOVE AND PERISH

## Ernest Dudley

In Castlebay, North Wales, Dick Merrill is on trial, accused of murdering his wife. Merrill, good looking and attractive, is fatally in love with Margot Stone, who is herself already married. Philip Vane, a lawyer whose career was mysteriously ruined, finds himself similarly infatuated with Margot when he becomes personally involved in Merrill's sensational murder-trial. A shadowy figure, Vane's participation in the trial is twisted and erratic — will the outcome be as unpredictable?

# FRAMED IN GUILT

## John Russell Fearn

William Barridge, meek and mild solicitor's clerk, is found lying on the floor of his employer's locked office with a knife in his back. But how could a man so innocuous have had any enemies . . . ? When Superintendent Henshaw investigates, however, it becomes evident that Barridge had mysterious dealings with his brother in Australia — and an association with an attractive potential divorcee. Added to the list of suspects is Henry Minton, Barridge's employer — the only person with a key to the locked office . . .

# THE CLEOPATRA SYNDICATE

## Sydney J. Bounds

Maurice Cole, the inventor of a mysterious new perfume, is found murdered. But his employer's only concern is to recover the stolen perfume . . . He hires Daniel Shield, head of I.C.E. — the Industrial Counter Espionage agency — who is aided by Barney Ryker and the beautiful Melody Gay. The trail leads them to Egypt, where Shield must find international criminal Suliman Kalif and recover the perfume before the Nile runs red with the blood of a Holy War.